To

Tamara

D0811163

Enid Blyton's

DON'T BE SILLY,
MR TWIDDLE!

First published 1971
This reprint 1989

Published by Dean, an imprint of
The Hamlyn Publishing Group Limited,
Michelin House,
81 Fulham Road,
London SW3 6RB,
England

ISBN 0 603 03280 X

Printed in Italy

Enid Blyton's
DON'T BE SILLY,
MR TWIDDLE!

DEAN

CONTENTS

CHAPTER I

DON'T BE SILLY, MR. TWIDDLE!

Once Mrs. Twiddle was in bed with a bad cold.

Mr. Twiddle was very sorry, and he said he would do what he could to help. But Mrs. Twiddle thought to herself that she wasn't sure if Twiddle's help would be much use.

"You tell Mrs. Minny, the woman who comes to do the washing to-day, to come up and see me," said Mrs. Twiddle, sneezing into her handkerchief. "She can do

everything for me, and cook your dinner, and do a bit of washing as well."

So Mrs. Minny went up to see Mrs. Twiddle, and the two of them planned out the day's work.

"If you can scrub the scullery floor, and cook a bit of dinner, and wash out that dirty sheet over there and sponge that oily mark out of Mr. Twiddle's coat, and see that the cat has her dinner, I think we'd be all right," said Mrs. Twiddle. "Could you do that, do you think?"

"Oh, yes ma-am, easily," said kind Mrs. Minny. "Mr. Twiddle doesn't need to do a thing."

They sent Mr. Twiddle out to the chemist's so that he would be out of the way, because very often when he wanted to be helpful, he wasn't at all. Then Mrs. Minny set to work to peel potatoes and make a pie, and scrub the scullery floor and do a bit of washing.

She hung the washed sheet out in the garden and she pegged up Mr. Twiddle's sponged coat on the line, too, so that they

would both dry in the wind. She took up Mrs. Twiddle's dinner on a tray and she gave Mr. Twiddle his as well. Then she washed up and said good-bye.

"Everything's done, ma'am," she said, "and I've left a cold supper in the larder. If Mr. Twiddle will just bring in the coat and the sheet off the line, when they're dry, that's all there is to do."

"Thank you, Mrs. Minny," said Mrs.

Twiddle. "I'm very grateful. I'll tell Mr. Twiddle."

"Well, after Mrs. Minny had gone, Mrs. Twiddle happened to look out of the window, and it was pouring with rain. The drops splashed down, and Mrs. Twiddle remembered the sheet and the coat hanging out on the line in the garden. She called loudly to Twiddle.

"Twiddle! Twiddle! Go out and bring in the sheet and the coat out of the wet."

Twiddle was asleep. He awoke with a jump and got up out of his armchair. "Bring in the sheep and goat?" he said, sleepily. "What sheep and goat, dear?"

Mrs. Twiddle called downstairs again, impatiently. "It's raining, Twiddle, that's why I want the sheet and the coat brought indoors. Go and bring them in."

Well, Twiddle still thought Mrs. Twiddle said "Sheep" and "Goat," and he was rather surprised. So he called up again. "Do you really mean the sheep and the goat?"

Mrs. Twiddle thought he said "the sheet and the coat," and answered crossly.

10

"Are you *trying* to be stupid, Twiddle? Is there anything funny about bringing in a sheet and a coat out of the rain? I don't want them to get wet."

Twiddle thought there was something extremely funny about bringing a sheep and a goat indoors, but he knew better than to say anything more to Mrs. Twiddle. He knew he had better do as he was told at once. So he went out of doors and looked round for the sheep and the goat.

There were two sheep and a goat in the field at the bottom of his garden. Mr. Twiddle sighed. The goat was tied up, but the sheep weren't. What a bother it all was! Why should Mrs. Twiddle take it into her head to want to be so kind to sheep and goats all of a sudden?

Twiddle undid the gate at the bottom of the garden. He untied the goat and led it indoors to the kitchen. The goat was surprised, but it didn't mind very much. It looked at the tablecloth, and thought it might do for a meal. Twiddle shut the door and went down the garden to fetch the two sheep in out of the rain.

It was easy enough to catch one, but the other was afraid of him and ran away. So Mr. Twiddle firmly led the first sheep into the kitchen, let it join the goat, and then shut the door on them. He went off to bring in the other sheep.

Now, Mrs. Twiddle was lying in bed, wondering if Twiddle had brought in the sheet and the coat quickly, before they were soaked. She heard a noise in the kitchen, and she called out:

"Twiddle! Twiddle!"

"Be-heeeee, hee!" said the goat pleasantly.

"Baa-haa-haa-haa!" said the sheep, nibbling at a fern in the window. Mrs. Twiddle lay and listened to this in astonishment. Was Twiddle trying to be funny?

"Stop that noise," she said sharply. "Did you bring in the sheet and the coat, Twiddle?"

"Ba-hah!" said the sheep politely.

"Be-hee-hee," bleated the goat.

Mrs. Twiddle felt very angry. "Twiddle!

Will you please stop being funny? I don't like it when you act the goat like that! I'm asking you a question."

"Ba-hah-haaaaa," said the sheep wisely, and pulled over the plant-pot.

"Bee-hee-hee," said the goat, and ate half the table-cloth. It pulled at it, and a jug of milk toppled over and fell with a crash to the floor. Mrs. Twiddle lay and listened in alarm. What in the wide world

was Twiddle doing? She began to think he must have gone mad.

"Twiddle! What ever are you doing?"

She heard a pattering of feet. The goat was frightened when the milk fell over and ran round the kitchen. It bumped into the sheep who at once jumped right over two pails and a chair, making a clatter. Mrs. Twiddle listened in amazement.

"Be-ha, hee, be-ha, hee!" she heard, as the goat and the sheep sang together in chorus.

"TWIDDLE! If you don't stop being funny this very minute, I'll come down and see what you're up to!" shouted Mrs. Twiddle. This threat usually made Mr. Twiddle stop anything, but it didn't stop the sheep or the goat. They had a very gay time chasing one another—at least, it was a gay time for the goat, who had discovered that a sheep was a nice solid thing to butt, so he kept on butting, and the sheep kept on trying to get away, and falling into everything it could.

Mrs. Twiddle could bear it no longer. She

got out of bed and put on her dressing-gown, telling herself all the things she would do to Twiddle when she got downstairs. She went down, with a terrible frown on her face.

The goat chose that moment to be very frisky, and when Mrs. Twiddle appeared at the kitchen door, looking nice and plump and round, he thought she might be another kind of sheep. So he went up to her and butted her hard. Mrs. Twiddle sat down very suddenly and screamed.

The outer door opened, and in came Twiddle with the other sheep. "This was a most tiresome sheep to catch," he began. "Get in—shoo!"

The sheep gambolled in, and the goat at once butted it. The sheep backed heavily into Twiddle and he sat down just as suddenly as Mrs. Twiddle had done. But Mrs. Twiddle was now getting up, and there was such an awful look in her eyes that Twiddle was quite frightened.

"Twiddle! WHAT is the meaning of this?" said Mrs. Twiddle, in such a terrible

15

voice that the sheep and the goat stopped capering about, and listened too.

"Meaning of what?" asked Twiddle, from the floor. "You told me to bring the sheep and the goat in out of the rain, didn't you?"

Mrs. Twiddle stared at Twiddle as if he was quite mad. "Twiddle — I said, bring in the *sheet* and the *coat*," said Mrs. Twiddle. "Have you no sense? Why should I want sheep and goats in my kitchen?"

"Well, I really didn't know, dear," said Mr. Twiddle, going very red. "Never mind, now, never mind — you get back to bed quickly, and I'll take these creatures to the field again, I'm so very sorry about it. I must be getting a bit deaf."

Before Mrs. Twiddle could say another word — and she had plenty to say — Twiddle opened the kitchen door, and shooed out the surprised sheep and goat. They scampered down the path to the field. Twiddle slammed the kitchen door and went with them. He felt that he really couldn't bear Mrs. Twiddle looking at

16

him like that for one minute more!

He stayed out quite a long time in the rain, hoping that Mrs. Twiddle would be asleep when he got in. He crept in quietly and took off his wet boots. He quietly put a few more coals on the fire. He sat down in his armchair and quietly picked up his newspaper.

"She's asleep," he said. "What a bit of luck! Perhaps when she wakes up, she'll think it's all a dream!"

17

But a voice came down the stairs at that moment.

"Twiddle! Is that you? Have you brought in the sheet and the coat as I told you?"

Well — will you believe it — Twiddle hadn't! So out he went again into the rain and unpegged them from the line, soaking wet. And, unless I'm very much mistaken, Twiddle will be in bed with a cold himself to-morrow. And what a lot of uncomfortable things Mrs. Twiddle will say to him if they both have colds in bed together! Poor old Twiddle.

CHAPTER II

OH, MR. TWIDDLE!

Mrs. Twiddle was very busy. She had the whole table spread with all kinds of things —needles, cottons, scissors, bits of silk, flowers, and goodness knows what else!

Mr. Twiddle looked at her. He badly wanted her to help him with the crossword puzzle in the newspaper, but he didn't like to ask her, because her mouth was full of pins.

"I'm always afraid she'll swallow the pins when she has so many between her lips like that," thought Twiddle. "I wonder what she's doing. She *has* got a mess out on the table."

He waited until Mrs Twiddle had taken the pins out of her mouth and used them. Then he spoke to her.

"What are you doing with all that mess on the table, wife?" he said.

"Gracious, can't you see!" said Mrs. Twiddle. "I'm putting a bit of extra trimming on my best hat. Look, it's got violets on one side, and I'm going to put these little pink roses on the other. Don't you think they'll look nice?"

"Well, it makes the hat look rather like a garden," said Mr. Twiddle. "How long will you be?"

"I've nearly finished," said Mrs. Twiddle. "Then I'll help you with that puzzle. I can see you're longing for a bit of help. Just go and get me that shirt of yours over there that I've washed for you. I'll sew the top button on whilst I think of it."

Twiddle fetched his blue shirt. Mrs. Twiddle quickly sewed on a button, then fluffed out the flowers on her best hat. She looked at it with pleasure.

"It's lovely," she said. "Now, Twiddle dear, you can do something for me whilst I clear up this mess, then I'll help you."

"What do you want me to do?" asked Twiddle. "Not chop wood or anything like that, I hope."

"No," said Mrs. Twiddle. "Just take this shirt out and hang it on the line to dry, and take my best hat and put it into the hat-box under my bed. By the time you've done that for me I'll be ready."

"Right," said Twiddle. He picked up the shirt and the hat and went out of the room.

Well, you know old Twiddle, don't you? So you can guess what he did! Yes, you're right—he took the hat out into the garden and pegged it carefully up on the line,

and he took his blue shirt and tucked it into the hat-box under the bed!

Then he went downstairs and beamed at his wife. She had cleared up the mess, and was ready to do the puzzle with him.

"Now look," she said, "here's the first thing we have to guess—the name of somebody silly. Seven letters it has to be, Twiddle."

"I know who that is!" said Twiddle, at once. "It must be old Meddle. He's silly enough."

"No—Meddle has six letters, not seven in his name," said his wife. "Guess again. Can it be Brer Rabbit—no, that's ten letters. Dear me, I can't think of the right answer at all. Let's guess the next bit."

As they were in the middle of the puzzle there came a knock at the door and Mrs. Jones put her head in and smiled at them.

"Mrs. Twiddle, I'm off to tea with Sally Simple. She told me to bring you with me if you'd like to come."

"Oh yes, I would!" said Mrs. Twiddle, jumping up at once. "I'll just get my hat.

I've finished trimming it and it looks lovely.
I shall so like wearing it to Sally's."

She rushed upstairs. She put on her best
coat, found her best gloves, and then pulled
out the hat-box from under the bed.

She opened it — and how she stared when
she saw Twiddle's blue shirt in there.
"Whatever's this in my hat-box?" she
cried, and she pulled out the shirt. "Good
gracious, Twiddle's mad! He's put his
damp shirt into my hat-box. Oh, if he's

squashed it on top of my best hat I'll beat him with the rolling-pin, really I will!"

She looked under the shirt, but there was no hat there. She looked on her dressing-table. No hat there. She looked on the top shelf of her wardrobe, where she kept her other hats. No—her best hat wasn't there either.

She ran downstairs to Twiddle and Mrs. Jones. "Twiddle! What did you do with my best hat? It isn't in the hat-box—and you've put your shirt there! You really are a silly man."

"But surely I put your hat there!" said Twiddle in alarm. "Yes, surely I did. You told me to. Are you *sure* I put the shirt there? You told me to hang it on the line. I feel sure I pegged it out in the garden."

"Well, come to the window, and we'll see if you pegged the shirt out there!" cried Mrs Twiddle, in a temper. "Didn't I just tell you it was in the hat-box! Twiddle, where did you put my best hat?"

Twiddle went to the window and looked out into the garden, quite expecting to see his blue shirt hanging on the line, in spite of what Mrs. Twiddle said. But you know what he saw, don't you? Mrs. Twiddle's best hat hanging there, being blown about in the wind!

He stared at it in horror. Oh dear, oh dear, whatever in the world would Mrs. Twiddle say? Mrs. Twiddle saw the look of dismay on his face, and she looked out of the window, too. When she saw her lovely

best hat hanging on the line she gave a scream of horror.

"Oh, you bad man! Oh, you dreadfully silly creature! You hung my best hat on the line and put your shirt in my hat-box! Twiddle, you want your ears boxed! You really do! I've a good mind to do it!"

Twiddle hurried out into the garden before Mrs. Twiddle could do what she said. His face was red. Why did he do things like this? Dear, dear, his wife would never forgive him for pegging out her best hat like that!

He took it in, and Mrs. Twiddle snatched it from him to see if the pegs had put it out of shape. But they hadn't. She threw his blue shirt to Twiddle.

"Do what you like with it!" she cried crossly. "It's no good my telling you to peg it on the line. Put it into the coal-scuttle if you like — or inside the oven, where you once put the clock! Really, you are the silliest fellow in the world!"

Poor Twiddle said nothing. He felt most uncomfortable, because Mrs. Jones was laughing. He picked up the newspaper to finish the puzzle by himself. Mrs. Twiddle stood in front of the looking-glass and pinned on her best hat.

"It looks simply beautiful, dear," said Mrs. Jones, admiringly. "Really, it does!"

Mrs. Twiddle felt pleased. She wasn't in a temper any more. She tapped Twiddle on the shoulder.

"There's a new ginger-cake for your tea in the larder," she said. "Finish your puzzle, and then put the kettle on to boil."

"I wish I could guess this bit," sighed Twiddle. "The name of somebody silly — with seven letters!"

"I know, I know!" cried Mrs. Twiddle, and she gave a little giggle.

"Who is it?" asked Twiddle.

You know what she answered, don't you! Yes, it was Mr. *Twiddle!*

CHAPTER III

MR. TWIDDLE'S PEAR

Once Mr. Twiddle went out walking by himself, for it was a very fine day indeed. Twiddle's feet got very hot walking, and he wished he had put on his big boots. He felt very thirsty, too, and wondered if Sally Simple would let him have a drink when he passed her house.

"I'll ask her," he thought. He walked along down the road and came to the shops. Next door to the boot-shop there was a fine pear-tree overhanging the street wall. On it were several green pears, nearly ripe. Mr. Twiddle stared at them in delight. Now a pear to eat, a nice juicy pear when he was almost dying of thirst, would be simply lovely.

He wondered if he could call in at the boot-shop and ask the man to let him have one of the pears off the pear-tree. But he didn't quite like to do that. So he stood at the door of the shop, and turned over the

boots that were for sale on a big stall in front of the door.

The shopman saw him and came forward. He bowed to Mr. Twiddle and spoke to him politely.

"What can I do for you this morning, sir? Would you like one of those pairs."

He meant, of course, would Twiddle like a pair of the boots and shoes he was looking at. But Twiddle's mind was full of the pears hanging over the wall. His heart gave a jump of joy when he heard the shopman say that, and he smiled all over his face.

"Would I like a pear!" he said, beaming. "I should just think I would! How nice of you to suggest it!"

"Well," said the shopman, "you're a very polite customer, I must say. Now, what kind of a pair would you like? What colour? Black or brown?"

Mr. Twiddle felt a bit puzzled. He hadn't heard of black pears before. He thought brown ones might be a bit over-ripe. So he looked at the shopman, and said: "Well, Mr. Shopman, I think I'd really rather have a yellow pear, if you don't mind. I always like them best!"

The shopman pursed up his lips and frowned. "Well, I'm sorry, sir, but I haven't a single yellow pair to-day," he said. "They're all black or brown. But come in this afternoon, and maybe I'll have one for you. I can send to the other end of the town to my brother. He may

have a fine yellow pair."

"Oh, pray don't bother to do that," said Mr. Twiddle. He looked at the green pears on the tree. "Er—well, a *green* pear would do quite well, you know. They're a little bit hard, that's the only thing. Yellow ones are so nice and soft."

The shopman began to think Mr. Twiddle was just a little mad. "I haven't any green pairs to-day," he said, gruffly. "You come along in an hour, and I'll have a yellow pair for you. What size would you like?"

"Oh—as large as possible, please," said Twiddle, eagerly, thinking how lovely it would be to sink his teeth into an enormous ripe yellow pear and taste the sweet juice.

The shopman looked down at Mr. Twiddle's feet. They didn't look very large to him.

"All right," he said. "A large yellow pair. And would you like a laced pair or a buttoned pair?"

Mr. Twiddle stared at the shopman, thinking that *he* must be a little mad. He had never in his life heard of a pear with laces or buttons. After all, if you wanted to, you took the skin off a pear—you didn't unbutton or unlace it. "He will be asking if I want hooks and eyes on it next," thought Twiddle. "Really, he is a most peculiar man."

"I don't think I want my pear laced *or* buttoned," said Twiddle. "Just plain, if you know what I mean."

"I see," said the shopman, not seeing at all. "Well—do you want a tongue?" Of course, he meant did Twiddle want a tongue inside his shoes—but Twiddle didn't know that. He stared again at the shopman, and felt a little angry.

"Do I want a *tongue*?" he said. "Well, haven't I been talking with my tongue all this time. Why should I want another. Look—here's mine! Good-bye! I'll come back in an hour's time for a nice yellow pear, without laces or buttons, and with NO tongue!"

Mr. Twiddle had put out his tongue to show the shopman he had one—and the shopman thought he was being rude. He gazed after Twiddle, and shook his head. "He seemed such a nice man at first," he said. "But he must be mad. Quite mad. Well—I'll send over to my brother's and see if he has got a nice yellow pair of boots or shoes without laces, buttons, or tongues!"

His brother did have a pair. They were bright yellow shoes with elastic sides. He was glad to get rid of them, because he hadn't been able to sell them. The shopman who had talked to Twiddle looked out for him in an hour's time — and sure enough, there he was, coming back to see if he really could have a nice juicy yellow pear!

"Good day again!" called the shopman. "I've got that yellow pair for you — just your size, too! Look!"

Twiddle stared in dismay at the bright yellow shoes. He simply couldn't bear them. He knew Mrs. Twiddle wouldn't like them either.

"Why are you offering me shoes?" he said, in astonishment. "I meant a pear to eat — you know, like those growing on that tree over there. I was thirsty. Couldn't you give me one of *those* pears, please? I don't want this pair of shoes. They are dreadful."

That made the shopman very angry. "They are fine shoes!" he cried. "You ordered them, didn't you? It's all very well for you to say you wanted a pear off that tree now — but what you asked me for was a pair of yellow shoes without laces, buttons or tongues. And here they are. Pay

me for them, please."

"Now look here, now look here," began Mr. Twiddle, feeling rather frightened. "This won't do. I'll buy a pear off your tree—but I won't buy those yellow shoes. How much will you charge me for a pear off the tree?"

"It's not my tree," said the shopman, and

he looked fiercely at Twiddle. "It doesn't grow in my garden. It grows next door. Now—what about these shoes? They cost one pound and they're a bargain. Pay up, please, or I'll have to go and tell that policeman over there that you've been making fun of me and won't pay my bill."

The policeman looked a bit fierce. Twiddle gave a deep sigh and felt in his pocket. He pulled out a handful of coins and showed them to the man. "That's all I've got," he said.

"Well, it's two and a half pence short," said the man. "But I'll let you off that. Do you want to put the shoes on now?"

"Oh no, thank you," said Mr. Twiddle, quickly. "No—I'll carry them."

So poor Twiddle went home with the bright yellow shoes and tried to hide them in the boot-cupboard right at the very back. But Mrs. Twiddle caught sight of them before he put them there, and called out in surprise.

"Twiddle! Are those yellow daffodils

you've got? Put them in water, my dear man—don't put them in the boot-cupboard!"

So poor Twiddle had to show Mrs. Twiddle the shoes—and I really couldn't tell you what she said. It would fill this whole book and then want a few more pages besides! He hasn't worn the shoes yet—and I don't somehow think he ever will. He does make some funny mistakes, doesn't he?

CHAPTER IV

MRS. TWIDDLE IS VERY CROSS

One day Mrs. Twiddle had a great deal to do, and when she had to rush here and there, she was not very good-tempered.

Usually Mr. Twiddle kept out of her way then. If he didn't he would be sent on this errand and that and kept very busy, too. He would be scolded if he forgot anything, and he didn't like that.

"Twiddle! Put down your paper and go and answer the door!" cried Mrs. Twiddle, rolling out some pastry with her rolling-pin.

"Twiddle! The fire is going down! Put some coal on it. Really, why you can't see for yourself that the fire is almost out, I cannot think!"

"Twiddle! You look even stupider than usual! Why don't you do something to help me!"

Poor Twiddle. He put down his paper. He ran here and there. He did his best to help.

Mrs. Twiddle went to the larder to get the tin of sugar. She screwed up her nose in disgust.

"Bother! The fish has gone bad. Twiddle, where are you? Bless the man, he's gone and put his hat on! Twiddle, you don't think you are going out, do you? Just when I'm so busy and want your help, too. *And* your best hat! Whatever makes you think I'll let you go out wearing your best Sunday hat on a busy morning like this? You must be mad."

39

"No, I'm not," said Twiddle. "I want to go and call on old Mrs. Jenks to see how she is, and my old hat really wants cleaning."

"What! Call on old Mrs. Jenks when I want you here! Twiddle, you are enough to drive anyone mad. Now, quick—take this bad fish and put it into the dustbin, and take off that best hat and put it back on the top shelf of the wardrobe. Hurry now!"

Twiddle sighed and tried to hurry. He took off his best hat. Mrs. Twiddle pushed the dish of bad fish into his hand. He turned to go out of doors to the dustbin.

"If only I could have slipped out when she wasn't looking!" thought Mr. Twiddle, as he took off the dustbin lid. He put in his best hat and slapped the lid on again. Then he went indoors.

He ran upstairs and put the dish of bad fish on the shelf in the wardrobe, where all the hats were kept. He was so busy thinking of how unlucky he was that morning that he didn't notice what he was doing at all.

That was exactly like Mr. Twiddle—the dearest, kindest old thing, but oh, the silly things he did!

"Now, Twiddle, go and sweep out the yard," said Mrs. Twiddle. "It's full of rubbish. Put it into the dustbin when you've finished."

Twiddle swept out the yard. He shovelled up the rubbish and popped it into the dustbin, all on top of his best hat. But he didn't know that.

Twiddle was glad when that day was over and he could go up to bed. He sank into his bed with a sigh and shut his eyes at once. But it wasn't long before Mrs. Twiddle sat up in bed and sniffed hard.

"What's the matter?" asked Twiddle, sleepily. "Are you starting a cold, sniffing like that?"

"I can smell a smell," said Mrs. Twiddle. "An awful smell."

"Well, never mind," said Twiddle. "Let it be. It won't hurt you. I can't smell a thing."

"Twiddle, sit up and sniff," said Mrs.

41

Twiddle, and she gave him a punch. "It's a terrible smell."

Twiddle groaned. He sat up and sniffed — and sure enough there really was a most peculiar and horrible smell in the bedroom. Whatever could it be?

"It's like fish," said Mrs. Twiddle.

"Impossible," said Twiddle.

"I know," said Mrs. Twiddle. "But it's exactly like very bad fish — very bad fish indeed. How very extraordinary!"

"Most," said Twiddle, and lay down again. But Mrs. Twiddle wasn't going to have that. No — that smell had got to be found. No doubt about that!

"Get up and see if you can find where the smell is coming from," said Mrs. Twiddle. So Twiddle got out of bed and sniffed hard again. It seemed to come from the wardrobe. He went over to it. He opened the door — and at once the smell came out, ten times stronger!

"Oooof!" said Mrs. Twiddle. "It must be something the cat's brought in! How simply disgusting! Twiddle, look in the wardrobe."

Twiddle looked. The smell seemed to come from the top shelf where the hats were kept. He stood on a chair and looked — and there, among the hats, was the dish of bad fish!

Twiddle stared at it in horror. How in the world could he have been so stupid as to put it there! He stood still for such a long time that Mrs. Twiddle grew impatient.

"What's the matter, Twiddle? What's in the wardrobe?"

"Fish," said Twiddle in a small voice.

"*Fish!*" said Mrs. Twiddle, not at all believing him. "Don't be silly. Fish couldn't get into the wardrobe."

"It *is* fish," said Twiddle. "I'll take it downstairs and put it into the dustbin. Most extraordinary thing. Never heard of such a thing in my life. Can't think what the cat's been up to, to take fish into the wardrobe."

"Nor can I," said Mrs. Twiddle, angry and puzzled. "Twiddle, it's cold to-night. Just put your best hat on, and your coat. I sent your old hat to be cleaned this afternoon."

Twiddle looked for his best hat. It wasn't there.

"It's not there," he said.

"It must be," said Mrs. Twiddle, impatiently. "You put it there yourself this morning. Find it at once, or I'll come and look for it!"

Twiddle turned pale. He suddenly knew what had happened. He must have put his best hat into the dustbin—and put the bad fish into the wardrobe. Mrs. Twiddle could wait to longer. She jumped out of bed and went to find Twiddle's hat.

She saw the dish of fish. She stared at Twiddle, and he stared back, red in the face now, instead of white! Poor Twiddle!

"Twiddle! The cat may be clever enough to carry fish to the wardrobe—but not on a dish! *You* must have put it there! Dreaming as usual! But oh, Twiddle, *don't* tell me you put that lovely best hat of yours into the dustbin?"

Twiddle didn't tell her. She knew! He went downstairs with the bad fish, and made his way out into the yard. The cat followed him, sniffing eagerly at the fish. Twiddle put the fish into the dustbin, and then looked for his hat. It was there, covered with rubbish, tea-leaves—and now fish!

Twiddle put the lid on the dustbin again. He didn't know that the cat had jumped in after the fish, and was shut in. He went sadly back to the bedroom, holding his hat in his hand. How it smelt!

Mrs. Twiddle said a lot to him, and he had to listen. It was a long time before he went to sleep. When he woke up he remembered what had happened.

"I must be very, very careful to-day," he thought. "I'll do nothing to make Mrs. Twiddle angry at all!"

So he was as good as he could be and Mrs. Twiddle was pleased — until she discovered the cat shut in the dustbin!

"So this is why you've been so good and quiet!" she scolded. "You'd shut the poor cat in the dustbin! You bad man! Twiddle, I've a good mind to shut you up in the dustbin too!"

She looked so fierce that Twiddle snatched a hat from the hallstand, and fled. It wasn't until he was a mile away that he found he had taken Mrs. Twiddle's old hat by mistake.

No wonder everyone laughed when he went by! He really is a funny fellow, isn't he?

CHAPTER V

MR. TWIDDLE AND THE BOOTS

Once Mrs. Twiddle turned out the landing cupboard, and she found two pairs of Mr. Twiddle's old boots. She took them down to the kitchen and looked at them.

"Well, they could really be mended," she said to herself. "They want new soles, but that's all. The heels are quite good, and so are the upper parts. In these hard days we mustn't throw old boots

away. I'll tell Twiddle to take them to be soled."

So when Twiddle came in from his walk, he saw the two pairs of old boots on the table. He looked at them in surprise.

"Fancy those old things turning up again!" he said. "I haven't seen them for years."

"They must be soled," said Mrs. Twiddle. "The soles are very bad. Look at them."

"Yes, so they are," said Twiddle, looking at the big holes in the soles. "All right, wife — they shall be sold."

Now Twiddle was making a very great mistake. He thought that Mrs. Twiddle meant him to *sell* the boots. When she said they must be soled, he thought she meant *sold*. She really meant that the soles must be mended, of course — but he didn't know that.

He wrapped the boots up in brown paper and set off down the road to the shop that bought old clothes. "I ought to get a nice lot of money for these boots," thought Twiddle, pleased. "What shall I buy with the money?

I want a new pipe, really. And Mrs. Twiddle could do with some boiled sweets. She does like them so much. And the cat could have a kipper. It has behaved quite well lately."

Mr. Twiddle sold the boots and with the money he got, he bought himself a fine new pipe.

He went to the sweetshop and bought a bag of sweets for Mrs. Twiddle. And he bought a kipper for the cat, so Twiddle had no money left by the time he got home.

He put down the sweets on the table. Mrs. Twiddle was delighted to see them. "Oh, thank you," she said. "That is kind of you. I thought you hadn't any money left this week."

"Well, I've just taken the boots to be sold," said Twiddle. "The man gave me the money!"

"But, Twiddle, why did the man give *you* money?" asked Mrs. Twiddle, thinking that the cobbler must have gone mad. After all, she always had to *pay* money to have her shoes mended — it seemed the

49

wrong way about for the man to pay Twiddle!

"Well, boots that are sold bring in money, don't they?" said Twiddle, thinking that his wife was being very stupid, all of a sudden. "Look—I got myself a new pipe, too."

Mrs. Twiddle stared at the fine pipe. She simply could *not* understand how it was that Twiddle had got money for taking boots to be mended!

"And I got a kipper for the cat, too," said Twiddle. "Puss, Puss, Puss!"

The cat jumped up at the kipper. Mrs. Twiddle really felt in a whirl. . . . Sweets for her—a pipe for Twiddle—and a kipper for the cat—all because she had sent Twiddle with two pairs of boots to be mended. Well, well, well!

Someone came to the back door just as Mrs. Twiddle was going to ask Twiddle a little bit more about it all. When she came back, Twiddle had gone out into the garden, and she forgot all about the affair until three days later.

Then she remembered the boots. She was just going out and she called to Twiddle. "Twiddle! Look after the kitchen fire for me. I'll be back soon. I'm going to get the groceries, and I shall call at the boot-shop for your two pairs of boots."

Twiddle stared at his wife in the greatest surprise. "Two pairs of boots!" he said. "That's funny! I've only *got* two pairs of boots—and one pair is on my feet, and the other is over there waiting to be cleaned."

"I mean the boots that are being mended," said Mrs. Twiddle.

"But there aren't any being mended," said Twiddle, wondering if his wife was quite well. "I tell you my boots are on my feet—and over there. Don't be silly, wife."

"Twiddle, I'll thank you not to call me silly," said Mrs. Twiddle, offended. "I know what I'm doing. If you've forgotten that there are boots of yours being mended, *I* haven't!"

She stalked out down the garden path, leaving Twiddle very puzzled. She went to the boot-shop and asked for Twiddle's boots.

"He brought two pairs here on Monday," she said. "They were to be soled, but not heeled. And by the way, did you give Mr. Twiddle money when he brought the boots to you? It seemed such a funny thing to me!"

The cobbler looked in surprise at Mrs.

Twiddle. "I didn't give Mr. Twiddle anything," he said, "and I haven't got his boots either. I don't know what you mean."

"But you *must* have his boots!" said Mrs. Twiddle. "I gave him two old pairs to bring here to be mended. Oh, please, do look for them! Maybe you've forgotten that he brought them."

The cobbler looked all round his shop. There were big boots and little ones there, but not Twiddle's. The cobbler shook his head.

"I'm quite certain that Mr. Twiddle didn't bring any boots here," he said. "He must have taken them to the other cobbler. I feel offended at that, Mrs. Twiddle, for you've dealt with me for years!"

He bent over his work, quite angry. Mrs. Twiddle blushed, for she hated anyone to be angry with her. She went out of the shop, furious with Twiddle, because she thought he had gone with his boots to the other cobbler's and hadn't told her. She hurried home as fast as she could go.

"Twiddle!" she cried, bursting into the

kitchen. "Twiddle! Why did you take your boots to the other cobbler on Monday, instead of to the one we always go to? Now you just tell me that!"

Twiddle really thought his wife had gone mad. Here she was talking about boots again! He thought he had better get her to bed and fetch the doctor. So he put his arm round her and tried to get her to the stairs. Mrs. Twiddle was really angry.

"Twiddle! Let go my arm! What do you mean by saying I must go to bed and see the doctor? It's *you* who ought to do that! You're losing your memory. You've forgotten already that you took those old pairs of boots to be soled on Monday!"

"Dear me, wife, I haven't forgotten that," said Twiddle, suddenly remembering. "I told you I'd taken them, didn't I? And I bought you some boiled sweets out of the money that the man gave me."

"He didn't give you any money!" cried poor Mrs. Twiddle. "He says he didn't. I asked him. Why do you tell me dreadful stories like that, Twiddle? To think we

have been married for thirty years and now
you are beginning to tell me stories!''

"I tell you, wife, I took those boots to
the old-clothes' shop, and I sold them, just
as you told me to," said Twiddle, quite in
despair. "I don't know why the man said
he didn't give me any money, but he did,
and I spent it all.''

Mrs. Twiddle stared at Twiddle, and
suddenly she knew what had happened.

She gave a groan that startled Twiddle very much.

"Oh, foolish man! Oh, stupid, ridiculous man! Oh, silly, silly man! I told you those boots were to be soled — s-o-l-e-d, Twiddle — and you went and sold them — s-o-l-d. I wanted you to get new soles put under them — and you go and sell them! Twiddle, will you ever, ever do anything really sensible? No — you never will!"

CHAPTER VI

MR. TWIDDLE AND THE BULBS

Now, one morning, when Mr. Twiddle was reading his paper, Mrs. Twiddle came bustling into the kitchen.

"Twiddle, when you go out shopping this morning, I want you to buy me two new bulbs, please."

"Certainly, my dear, certainly," said Mr. Twiddle, still reading his paper.

"We'd better have big ones," said Mrs. Twiddle. "They are much better really, though the small ones are cheaper."

"Right," said Mr. Twiddle, still reading his paper, and not taking very much notice.

There was a clatter as Mrs. Twiddle popped out to the dustbin, took off the lid, and threw something into the bin with a noise like glass. It was the two electric light bulbs that were no good.

The kitchen one had gone, and so had the bedroom one. Mrs. Twiddle did hope that Twiddle would remember to buy new ones when he was out.

"I suppose you mean to read your paper till it's one o'clock and the shops are shut?" she said, after a while.

"No, my dear, certainly not," said Mr. Twiddle, hurriedly looking at the clock. "Half past twelve! Dear me, I'd better go. Now let me see—fish for supper, change your library book, and er-er—what else was it, dear?"

"Bulbs," said Mrs. Twiddle, banging her iron down on the table. "BULBS, Twiddle. I knew you weren't listening to me, I knew . . ."

"All right, my dear, all right," said Twiddle, and hurried off with the shopping basket before his wife could say a word more. He bought the fish, and he changed her library book, then he stood and wondered what the third thing was.

"Ah, of course—bulbs," he said to himself. "Now what sort of a shop do I buy bulbs at? The flower-shop, I suppose. They grow bulbs in pots and bowls, so I expect

they have some to sell loose."

He went to the flower-shop and the girl came forward, and asked what he wanted.

"I want two bulbs," said Mr. Twiddle.

"What kind?" asked the girl. "It's a bit late for bulbs really, you know. You ought to have planted them before this."

"Oh," said Mr. Twiddle. "Well — Mrs. Twiddle didn't say what kind she wanted. What kind can I have?"

"Well, there are little ones, like snow-drops," said the girl, "and big ones, like daffodils and hyacinths. And middle-size like tulips."

"Ah — Mrs. Twiddle said two big ones," said Twiddle, remembering. "I'll have two of your biggest, please."

The girl picked him out two big daffodil bulbs. "These will be a brilliant yellow," she said. "You will be sure to keep them nice and wet, won't you? Water them once a week in their pot."

"Right," said Mr. Twiddle, and took the bag in which the girl had put the bulbs. He paid for them and went home, pleased that he had remembered everything.

"Well, you haven't been as long as usual," said Mrs. Twiddle. "I suppose you didn't meet any of your friends this morning!"

"Well, no, I didn't," said Twiddle, putting the things down on the kitchen table. "Here's the fish — and there's the book — and here are the bulbs. I got two nice big ones."

"Good," said Mrs. Twiddle. "Would you like to put them in for me? One is for the kitchen and one for the bedroom."

"I'll have to get two pots, then," said Twiddle, and trotted out to the shed.

Mrs. Twiddle stared after him in surprise. "Did he say he'd have to get two *pots*?" she said. "I couldn't have heard him right. After all, he has only got to stand on a chair and slip the bulb into the light for me."

Twiddle went out and found two pots. He set a daffodil bulb in each of them. He carried them back into the house and put one pot on the kitchen window-sill and one on the sill in the bedroom.

"I've put the bulbs in for you!" he shouted to Mrs. Twiddle, who was in the drawing-room.

"Thank you!" cried Mrs. Twiddle.

"They will be a brilliant yellow," called Mr. Twiddle.

Mrs. Twiddle thought he meant that the electric light bulbs would give a brilliant yellow light. "Good," she said, coming into the kitchen. "We shan't need to sit in the dark now!"

Twiddle stared at Mrs. Twiddle. That seemed a queer sort of remark to him, but he thought it must be a joke, so he laughed heartily. "Ha, ha, ha!"

Mrs. Twiddle didn't quite know why Twiddle was laughing, but she liked him to laugh, so she laughed, too.

"You must water them once a week," said Twiddle. Mrs. Twiddle stopped laughing, and looked at Twiddle in surprise.

"Water *what* once a week?" she asked at last.

"The bulbs, of course," said Twiddle.

"Don't be silly," said Mrs. Twiddle. Twiddle looked offended.

"I'm not silly," he said. "The girl in the shop said we were to water them once a week."

"I don't mind you being funny, but I don't like you to be silly," said Mrs. Twiddle sharply.

"All right, all right," said Mr. Twiddle, and he said no more, thinking that probably Mrs. Twiddle knew more about whether to water bulbs or not than the girl in the shop did.

Neither of them said a word more about the bulbs. But when evening came and it was dark in the kitchen Mrs. Twiddle got up to switch on the electric light. Nothing happened. No light came. Mrs. Twiddle looked at the light. There was no bulb there!

"I thought you said you had put the

bulbs in for me," she said to Twiddle.

"So I did, my dear; so I did," said Twiddle surprised.

"Well, I can't see a bulb," said Mrs. Twiddle, screwing up her eyes and looking at the light that wasn't there.

"It's on the window-sill," said Twiddle.

"Twiddle! Why on the *window-sill*?" asked Mrs. Twiddle. "Are you mad? I can't see the bulb on the window-sill."

"Well, only because it's in the *earth*," said Twiddle.

"In the *earth*?" said Mrs. Twiddle, wondering if Twiddle really had gone mad. "Why should you put a bulb in the earth?"

Twiddle thought Mrs. Twiddle was being terribly stupid. "To make it grow, of course," said Twiddle.

Mrs. Twiddle looked closely at the window-sill and she saw the pot of earth there. She stared at it, and then stared at Twiddle. A funny look came over her face.

"Twiddle," she said, "I suppose you knew I wanted those bulbs to put into the electric lights, didn't you?"

Twiddle stared at Mrs. Twiddle, and he suddenly felt very uncomfortable. Oh — how very, very awkward! So he had got the wrong kind of bulbs! Dear, dear, he was always doing things like that. Now what would Mrs. Twiddle say? She would go on and on the whole of the evening.

But she didn't. She suddenly began to laugh, and when Mrs. Twiddle laughed, everyone else had to laugh too, especially Twiddle.

"Oh — now I know why you wanted me to water the light once a week!" laughed Mrs. Twiddle. "Oh, Twiddle, you'll be the death of me, really you will! Well — you'll have to sit in the dark all the evening, that's all. If you *will* buy daffodil bulbs instead of electric light bulbs, I just can't help it!"

So they sat in the dark, and chuckled whenever they thought of the bright yellow daffodils that would grow from the brown bulbs. Funny old Twiddle — he does get things wrong if he can, doesn't he?

CHAPTER VII

MR. TWIDDLE AND THE
TOOTH-PASTE

Mr. Twiddle cleaned his teeth well every night and morning. He had a blue tooth-brush, and Mrs. Twiddle had a yellow one.

Mr. Twiddle liked tooth-paste in a tube and Mrs. Twiddle liked it in a tin. So they couldn't possibly mistake each other's brushes or tooth-paste when they cleaned their teeth.

Now one night Mr. Twiddle found that he had squeezed every scrap of tooth-paste out of his tube. So he called to his wife from the bathroom:

"My love! Will you get me some more tooth-paste to-morrow? Mine's finished."

"I don't see why you can't remember to get it yourself," said Mrs. Twiddle. "You pass the chemist's each morning when you fetch the paper."

"Well, I *will* get it then," said Twiddle.

"You'll never remember," said Mrs. Twiddle. "I know you, Twiddle! If you had to get your own tooth-paste you'd never have any to clean your teeth with for the rest of your life."

"What an untruthful thing to say!" said Twiddle, feeling quite cross, especially as he knew it was very likely true. He did have a very bad memory. "A most untruthful and ridiculous thing to say. I shall buy some to-morrow."

But he didn't buy any. He passed the chemist's on his way to fetch the paper, but he didn't think about tooth-paste at all, although one side of the window was filled with nothing but different kinds of tooth-paste!

So, that night, he again took up the empty tube and squeezed it. "Bother!" he thought. "I didn't get the tooth-paste! Well, I shan't say a word."

He didn't. But Mrs. Twiddle did. "I hope your new tooth-paste is all right," she called slyly, knowing perfectly well that Twiddle hadn't bought any.

"I am going to buy some to-morrow," said Twiddle in rather a high-and-mighty voice.

He went to get his paper as usual the next day, and when he came to the chemist's he stopped.

"Now, what was I going to buy here?" he wondered. "What was I going to buy? A razor-blade? A bottle of cough mixture? Some black-currant lozenges?"

He went in and bought all of them,

thinking that one of them must be right. Mrs. Twiddle smiled to herself when she saw what he had bought.

"You've decided not to clean your teeth with tooth-paste after all!" she said, in a polite sort of voice. "I see you have been to the chemist's and bought quite a lot of things — but not tooth-paste."

Twiddle felt so angry with himself that he nearly boxed his own ears. He went very red and Mrs. Twiddle laughed.

"I'll buy some for you myself this afternoon," she said. So she did, because she had a very good memory, and hardly ever forgot to do what she said she would.

She came in at tea-time with her shopping in a basket. She went to put the kettle on and then she unpacked her shopping.

"There's your tooth-paste," she said, picking up a long tube. "And here are some buns for tea. And here's a new pair of brown laces for you — and please put them into your brown shoes, not your black ones — and here's some glue to mend that broken teapot spout — and here's a new book from the library—and I've remembered to get you the soap you like."

"Thank you, my love," said Twiddle, wishing he had as good a memory as his wife had.

"Now do take the things that belong to you and put them away," said Mrs. Twiddle.

But, of course, Twiddle didn't. He left the laces and everything else on the side-table, and Mrs. Twiddle felt quite impatient when she saw them there.

"Now he'll forget where he put the laces and the tooth-paste," she thought. "Well, well—I shan't put the laces in his shoes for him and I shan't take his tooth-paste upstairs. He really must learn to do little things for himself."

So, when Twiddle came to do his teeth again that night, once more he found that all he had on the shelf was an empty tube, quite squeezed out.

"Now let me think," he said to himself. "Just let me think. I *have* got some tooth-paste now. Mrs. Twiddle got it for me. It isn't here. So it must still be downstairs on

70

the little table. I'll go and get it before she asks me if I've cleaned my teeth."

So Mr. Twiddle crept downstairs in the dark, went to the little table in the kitchen and groped about for the tooth-paste tube.

Soon he went upstairs again, very quietly, holding a tube in his hand. He didn't know he had the tube of glue instead of the tube of paste. He had quite forgotten that Mrs.

Twiddle had bought him some glue to mend the old teapot for her.

"Twiddle! Are you cleaning your teeth properly to-night?" called Mrs. Twiddle from the bedroom.

"Yes, dear, of course!" answered Twiddle, taking off the top of the tube of glue and squeezing some glue on to his tooth-brush.

"Funny colour!" he thought, when he saw it. "Not the same as usual. And what a nasty fishy smell! I wish I had gone to buy the tooth-paste myself. Mrs. Twiddle hasn't bought the kind I usually have."

He began to rub his teeth with it. Oh, what a dreadful taste! Twiddle couldn't bear it. He tried to open his teeth to rinse his mouth with water.

But to his amazement and horror he couldn't get his teeth apart. No wonder, because the glue was sticking them fast together!

"Twiddle! Aren't you ever coming to bed?" called Mrs. Twiddle, impatiently.

"Ooogle-oo-oo," said Twiddle, trying to

say "Just coming!" His lips seems to be sticking together now, too. Whatever could be the matter?

"What did you say, Twiddle?" called Mrs. Twiddle, astonished.

"Ug-ug-ug-ug," answered Twiddle, feeling really alarmed now.

"Twiddle! Speak up! Don't mumble like that," said Mrs. Twiddle, sharply.

"Oooph, oooph, ug," said Twiddle, and looked at himself in the mirror in fright.

Why couldn't he talk? Why couldn't he open his mouth? Whatever was happening?

"Do you think you're being funny, Twiddle?" cried Mrs. Twiddle, beginning to get cross.

Twiddle didn't think he was being funny at all, but he did think he was being very queer. He worked his lips about, trying to open them. But they were stuck fast.

Mrs. Twiddle jumped out of bed. She wasn't going to let Twiddle behave like that to her — mumbling and muttering instead of giving her a proper answer. She came sailing into the bathroom in her dressing-gown, looking so furious that Twiddle felt quite frightened.

"Twiddle! What is the matter with you? Answer me at once!" said Mrs. Twiddle.

But that was more than poor Twiddle could do. He stared forlornly at Mrs. Twiddle, and then tried to open his mouth by pulling at his stuck-together lips with his fingers, making a curious gurgling noise as he did so.

"The man's gone mad!" said Mrs.

74

Twiddle in fright. "Oh dear — I'd better get the doctor!"

But before she went to get him she had a look round the bathroom — and there, on the shelf, lay the tube of glue, a little golden drop oozing out of the tip. Mrs. Twiddle picked it up and looked at it. Then she looked at Twiddle. Then she picked up his tooth-brush and felt it. The bristles stuck to her fingers!

"Twiddle," said Mrs. Twiddle. "Oh, Twiddle! First you can't remember to buy yourself tooth-paste — then I buy it for you — and yet you go and clean your teeth with the glue I bought to mend the teapot spout. Twiddle, are you mad or just plain silly? What am I to do with you?"

Twiddle stared at the tube of glue in horror. His eyes looked ready to drop out of his head. So that was why it smelt so fishy? Good gracious, he had stuck his teeth and lips together and perhaps he would never be able to get them unstuck again. Mrs. Twiddle always bought such strong glue!

"You'd better come to bed before you do anything else silly," said Mrs. Twiddle. "Come along. You'll be washing your face with the tooth-paste and brushing your hair with the bathroom stool if I leave you for a moment!"

Mr. Twiddle got into bed, very sad and very much alarmed. It was awful to have to listen and listen to Mrs. Twiddle and not be able to answer back at all. He felt so bad about it after half an hour of listening that some big tears rolled down his cheeks.

And there must have been something very strong in poor Mr. Twiddle's tears, because the drops unstuck the glue on his lips and teeth, and he was able to open his mouth again and speak! Oh, how glad he was. He sat up in bed and opened and shut his mouth like a goldfish.

"Ooooph!" said Twiddle, finding his voice again. "One more word from you, Mrs. Twiddle, and I get the glue and stick *your* lips together. Just one more word!"

And Mrs. Twiddle was so astonished to hear Twiddle talk to her like that that she didn't say another word; so Twiddle was able to go peacefully to sleep after he had washed his lips and teeth well to get rid of the taste of glue.

But Mrs. Twiddle did have the last word, of course, the next day. She gave Twiddle the teapot to mend and handed him two tubes — the tube of tooth-paste and the tube of glue.

"You probably want to use your tooth-paste instead of the glue to stick on the spout," she said, in a polite voice. "So here are both. Use which you like."

And that annoyed Twiddle so much that he actually thought about what he was doing, and mended the spout really well — with the glue!

CHAPTER VIII

MR. TWIDDLE LETS THE CAT IN

"Twiddle, dear, let the cat out, will you?" said Mrs. Twiddle, busily knitting in her chair by the fire.

"I don't know why you can't teach that cat to open the doors," grumbled Mr. Twiddle, getting up. "You always say she's so very, very clever—and yet she has never learnt a simple thing like that!"

"Well, she's very sharp, the way she goes and sits by the door whenever she wants to come in or out," said Mrs. Twiddle. "Do hurry, Twiddle."

"I shall keep the cat waiting if I like," said Mr. Twiddle, who had never been able to like his wife's cat. He stopped to take something out of a drawer. The cat miaowed.

"Don't call me names!" said Twiddle. "You're a most annoying creature. When you're out you want to come in, and when you're in, you want to go out. I know you! You just want to go and have a chat with the

cat next door, so you make me get up and let you out—and then when you find the cat next door isn't there, you'll want me to get up and let you in. You're a nuisance."

"Miaow!" said the cat, and began to wash herself. Mr. Twiddle opened the door, but the cat went on washing herself.

"Look at that now!" said Twiddle, exasperated. "Asking to go out and she doesn't want to after all! All right, I'll shut the door, Puss, and next time you want to go out you can WAIT!"

He shut the door, but before it was quite closed the cat slipped out like a shadow, and the tip of her tail was caught in the door. She gave such an anguished yowl that Mrs. Twiddle leapt out of her chair.

"Twiddle! How cruel you are! You shut the cat in the door!"

"I did not," said Twiddle, a little scared himself by the cat's dreadful yowl. "She slid out as I was shutting the door and the tip of her tail got pinched, that's all. Serve her right."

"I will not have you talk like that," said Mrs. Twiddle, getting all upset, and dropping a stitch in her knitting.

"Well, we'll not talk any more about it," said Twiddle, sitting down with his newspaper again. "There's no more to be said."

But there was, because Mrs. Twiddle had a great deal to say. By the time she had finished Mr. Twiddle was certain that he was the cruellest man in the world, and that he had upset his wife enough to make her feel quite ill, and had half-killed the poor, dear cat.

"And now I suppose you won't get her in to-night," said Mrs. Twiddle, a tear dropping on to her knitting. "You'll make her stay out in the cold."

"I will get her in," said kind-hearted Mr. Twiddle, who really couldn't bear to see his wife upset. "I'm sorry I pinched her tail. I promise you I'll get her in to-night."

"Thank you, Twiddle," said Mrs. Twiddle in a small voice, and smiled at him. After that he read his newspaper in peace, and forgot all about the cat till Mrs. Twiddle said it really was time for bed. She put away her knitting and got up.

"You'll get the cat in, dear, won't you?" she said.

"Oh dear me, the cat, yes, I'll get her in," said Twiddle. "You go on up."

"Open the scullery door, dear, and she'll come in there and go straight to her basket by the copper," said Mrs. Twiddle. "There are mice there, and I like her to sleep there

81

now instead of here in the kitchen."

"Right," said Twiddle, and opened the door for Mrs. Twiddle to go upstairs. Then he yawned, made up the fire to keep in for the night, and wound up the clock. Then he went out of the kitchen into the scullery and opened the door.

No cat came sliding in by his legs. He called loudly. "Puss, Puss, Puss! Come along! Puss, Puss!"

No puss came. Mr. Twiddle waited for about three minutes, till he felt rather cold. Then he called again, rather impatiently.

"Puss! PUSS! Don't you hear me? Come along in at once."

No cat appeared. Mr. Twiddle began to wish he hadn't promised to let her in that night. Suppose the cat kept him standing there for an hour? It would be just like her. She was probably hiding in a bush just outside, laughing to herself to see him standing there waiting. Twiddle felt angry.

Then an idea came to him. He would tempt the cat in. He went to the larder and found the fish for breakfast, three nice herrings. He took one, wrapped it up in a newspaper and then laid it on the mat just inside the scullery door. Then he went back to the warm kitchen and sat down with his paper again, to wait for the cat to come in. He was sure he would hear the rustling of the paper, as the cat tried to get at the herring.

Then he meant to hop up, shut the door

and put the fish back into the larder! Such a nice, simple plan, thought Mr. Twiddle. As indeed it was.

Unfortunately, Mr. Twiddle fell sound asleep as soon as he got back into his chair. He didn't hear the cat come in and fiddle at the paper round the fish. He didn't hear the next-door cat come in, too, and get excited about the herring. He didn't even hear the ginger cat across the road walk in, or the big tabby from the bottom of the garden.

Mrs. Twiddle's cat was angry to think she might have to share the herring with the others. She spat and hissed at them. Then in walked Black Tom, the biggest cat in the town, and all the others made way for him.

Black Tom began to tear at the paper. The other cats came closer. He hit out at them. The tabby hit back, spitting and snarling. Then, quite suddenly, all the cats exploded together into one big hiss of anger.

The noise awoke Mr. Twiddle. He sat

up and remembered his plan of getting the cat indoors. "She's there now," he thought to himself. "How clever I am! I'll just pop the fish back into the larder, and shut the scullery door. Hi, Puss, is that you?"

All the five cats heard his voice and became quiet. They hid in different places as he came out into the dark scullery. He groped about for the fish and found it on the floor, its paper almost off. He popped it into the larder, and spoke to the cat.

"Now you settle down and go to sleep, Puss! No more going in and out to-night!"

He went back into the kitchen. Unfortunately, he had left the larder door open, and the cats soon found this out. As soon as Twiddle was safely upstairs in bed, Black Tom led the way to the fish-smell in the larder. The parcel of herrings was dragged down with a thud. A small dish came with it and broke on the floor. The cats spat at one another.

Mrs. Twiddle awoke with a jump, when the dish broke. She sat up in bed and listened. She couldn't make out what the noise downstairs was at all.

She clutched poor Twiddle and woke him up with a start. "Twiddle! It's burglars! They're downstairs."

Twiddle had often been awakened by

Mrs. Twiddle and told there were burglars. But there never had been and he was getting tired of going downstairs for nothing. He turned over and settled himself comfortably again.

"Rubbish!" he said, sleepily. "You're imagining things as usual."

Pssssssssssssst! went the cats, and one of them gave a frightful howl. Mr. Twiddle sat up with a jump, and Mrs. Twiddle groaned in fright.

"Twiddle! You simply must go down and see what it is!" whispered Mrs. Twiddle. Twiddle didn't want to in the least. But he had to pretend to be brave even if he didn't feel it, so down he went, with a poker in one hand and a hammer in the other.

The noise came from the scullery. Mr. Twiddle switched on the light suddenly, and then stood still in horror at the scene. The place was full of cats! They chewed and hissed, gnawed and spat! Mr. Twiddle went suddenly mad with rage.

He leapt at them, dealing out slaps and

blows with his bare hand, for even in his rage he felt he couldn't use the poker or the hammer. The cats began to yowl and snarl, almost falling over one another, trying to get away from the angry man.

"Brrrrr! That's for you! Grrrrr! Take that. How dare you come into my house! Out of my way, out of my way! I'll teach you to come here in the middle of the night!"

Mrs. Twiddle, trembling upstairs, felt certain that Mr. Twiddle must be dealing with at least five dangerous burglars. How brave of him! How marvellous he was! Then she heard the scullery door open and then shut again with a bang.

After that Mr. Twiddle came upstairs, panting and angry. Mrs. Twiddle greeted him with open arms.

"Twiddle, dear! How brave you are! Are you hurt? How many were there?"

"Five at least," said Twiddle, "probably seven or eight. Anyway, I've dealt with them and sent them all flying."

"I think you're marvellous," said Mrs. Twiddle, still thinking that Mr. Twiddle had fought burglars. Mr. Twiddle was pleased and surprised at his wife's admiration.

"I went for them like anything," he said. "You should have seen them rush out of the scullery door, tails out behind them!"

Mrs. Twiddle felt astonished. "Tails?" she said. "Did you say tails? How could they have tails?"

"Well, don't cats generally have tails?" said Mr. Twiddle.

"Cats! Were they cats? I thought they were burglars!" cried Mrs. Twiddle.

"Of course they were cats," said Mr. Twiddle crossly. "I suppose that stupid animal of yours brought them all in. They've eaten practically everything in the larder."

"Oh! How wicked! How dreadful!" cried Mrs. Twiddle. "Oh, Twiddle, I do hope you gave our puss a smacking, too, and sent her out. I hope you didn't let her in again."

"I did not," said Mr. Twiddle. "I had great pleasure in smacking her. Now perhaps you won't make me keep getting up to go and let her in and out."

"I certainly won't," said Mrs. Twiddle, very angry indeed to think that her petted, spoilt cat should actually have dared to fill the scullery with her friends and raid the larder.

Well, well, well! Puss could certainly stay out all night.

Twiddle fell asleep and snored a little. Mrs. Twiddle lay and thought about the cats. Then she suddenly sat up and poked Twiddle hard.

"Twiddle! There's something I want to know. *Who* left the larder door open, so that the cats got in?"

But Twiddle was not going to answer questions like that. Not he! He snored a little louder, and made no movement at all. Leave that till the morning! Perhaps Mrs. Twiddle would forget about it by then.

But she won't! It's quite certain she will remember to ask Twiddle that question, and a lot more besides. Poor Twiddle—he does get himself into trouble, doesn't he?

CHAPTER IX

MR. TWIDDLE DOESN'T LIKE THE CAT

"Now, Twiddle," said Mrs. Twiddle one morning, when she had had a letter from her cousin Amanda, "I think I shall have to go away for a day or two, because my cousin Amanda is ill and needs someone to look after her."

"But I can't do without you," said Twiddle, quite alarmed at being left on his own. "Who will get my breakfast? And make the bed? And light the kitchen fire when it goes out?"

"You will, Twiddle dear," said Mrs. Twiddle. "It's time you learnt to do a few things for yourself. It won't hurt you, and I shan't be gone long. Now, cheer up and don't look so alarmed."

"Will you take the cat with you?" asked Twiddle. He didn't like the cat, and the cat didn't like him. "I don't feel as if I can possibly look after the cat."

"Well, you must," said Mrs. Twiddle firmly. "Of course I shan't take her with me. I shouldn't think of such a thing. Don't be silly. The cat's no trouble."

"It's no trouble to you, but it's a great trouble to me," said Twiddle, thinking of the many times that the cat had tripped him up, jumped on to his middle when he was asleep, and stolen fish of all kinds that he was going to have for breakfasts or suppers. "That cat is a great nuisance. I shall not look after her."

"You are not to talk like that, Twiddle," said Mrs. Twiddle, in such a sharp voice that Twiddle thought he really had better not say any more. But he was very upset to think that Mrs. Twiddle was going away and leaving him to look after himself—and the cat.

Mrs. Twiddle packed a small bag, and told Twiddle to remember ever so many things.

"The milkman has been, so there is plenty of milk for your tea. The baker will come soon. There is a herring for your supper, and a kipper for your breakfast. You know how to fry them because you have seen me do it plenty of times. There are two eggs in the larder as well, so you can have those if you want to."

"Yes, love," said Twiddle, trying hard to remember everything.

"And don't forget to give the cat her milk each day, and to get her into the house at night," said Mrs. Twiddle. "And *don't* let her sleep on the beds."

"Certainly not," said Twiddle, quite determined about that. "Well, I hope Amanda will soon be better, my dear, so that you can come back home. I shall miss you very much."

"Good-bye, Twiddle dear," said Mrs. Twiddle, "and don't leave the front door open when you go out, and don't let the kitchen fire out if you can help it, and don't leave the taps running, and don't— "

"You'll miss your bus," said Twiddle, who didn't like all this don't-ing. "Good-bye, love, take care of yourself."

Mrs. Twiddle went, and Twiddle trotted

off into the scullery to do the washing-up.
The cat was sitting on the window-sill
there, washing herself.

"You're always washing yourself," said
Twiddle. "Can't think why. You don't get
as dirty as all that. Now you listen to me,
Cat—I've got to look after you—but any
nonsense from you and you'll get spanked."

"Ss-ss-sss," said the cat, rudely.

"Don't hiss at me like that," said Twiddle,

running the hot water into the bowl. The cat watched him. Then she jumped down, rubbed against his legs, and mewed.

"What are you doing that for?" asked Twiddle. "You only do that when you want something. You've had your milk. I saw Mrs. Twiddle giving it to you."

The cat gave up rubbing against Twiddle's legs, because he kept pushing her away. She strolled to the kitchen, which was empty. She jumped up on to the breakfast-table.

The jug of milk was still there. The cat began to lick, trying her hardest to reach the milk. When she had licked a little of it, she put up her paw to try and get the milk nearer—and over went the jug!

The milk streamed over the table. The cat was pleased. Now there was plenty! She began to lick it up.

Twiddle heard the noise of the falling jug and came to see what it was. He was very angry when he saw the spilt milk and the spoilt tablecloth. He tried to smack the cat, but she put out a paw and gave him a sharp scratch, then leapt out of the window.

"Bother the thing!" said Twiddle, annoyed. He bathed the scratch, and then went on with the washing-up. When he had done that he tidied the kitchen, and swept the scullery. Then he felt very tired and went to sit down in his armchair. He took up the paper—but he didn't read much of it because he was soon asleep. Mrs. Twiddle said that Twiddle could go to sleep at any

hour of the day, and this was quite true.

Twiddle was really enjoying his nap when something landed with a jerk right on to his middle, and then settled down heavily, digging pins into him all the time. He woke up with a jump.

The cat was lying peacefully on him, digging her claws in and out, purring loudly, very comfortable and happy. Twiddle was very angry. He tried to shake the cat off, but she clung to him with all her claws.

"How many times have I told you not to jump on me like that?" shouted Twiddle, in a fine old rage. "You make me into a sort of bed for yourself, and always wait till I'm asleep before you jump. I won't have it!"

He shook the cat off at last, shooed her to the door and slammed it behind her. Then he settled down again. But the cat came in at the window, waited by the fire till Twiddle was sound asleep and snoring a little, and then jumped up on to his middle once more. Twiddle awoke again with a jump, and the cat leapt off.

Poor Twiddle! He decided not to sleep

any more. The cat didn't mean to let him, anyway. Twiddle went to the larder and wondered what to have for his dinner. The baker came whilst he was wondering, and Twiddle went to get the bread from him. He left the larder door open.

The cat went in, and smelt the herring and jumped up to the shelf at once. The next thing that Twiddle saw was the cat dragging his precious herring over the floor and out of the door. He was just too late to stop her.

"Look at that cat!" he said to the baker. "She's the most annoying, interfering cat you ever saw. I suppose you don't want a cat, do you?"

"Well, I've rats in the bakery," said the baker. "I don't mind having her. If she'll catch them I'll keep her."

"Well, you can have her and welcome," said Twiddle. He ran after the cat, pounced on her and popped her into a sack. The baker put her into his cart and drove off. Twiddle was very pleased.

"Now that cat can't interfere with me any

more," he said, rubbing his hands together. "I shall have to have the kipper for my supper, now that she has stolen the herring. And I'll have an egg for my breakfast."

Twiddle thought it was very nice without the cat. He could leave the larder door open if he wanted to. He could leave the milk on the table. He could go to sleep without being waked up with a jump.

When his supper-time came he cooked the kipper.

It smelt good. He put it on a plate and carried it carefully to the kitchen. But suddenly he tripped over something and fell down with a crash. The plate broke. The kipper shot into the air and disappeared. Twiddle banged his head hard against the wall.

"Miaow!" said a voice, and Twiddle saw the cat sitting down in the passage, looking at him.

"So it was *you* that tripped me up, was it?" said Twiddle, very angry, and most surprised to see the cat there after he had given it to the baker. "What have you come

back again for? Hi—leave that kipper alone!"

The cat had suddenly smelt the kipper, which had landed on a nearby chair. It jumped up and pounced on it. It fled out of the door with it.

"Well, it looks as if I'm never going to have any meals in this house whilst that cat's about," thought poor Twiddle. "Herring gone — kipper gone — it's too bad."

Twiddle was so angry that when it was time to lock up the house, he didn't open the door and call the cat in, as he usually did. No — let it stay out in the cold, the horrid, thieving animal! It ought to be sitting in the bakery, catching mice.

So the cat was left out and Twiddle went to bed. He fell asleep and had an awful dream. He dreamt that somebody made him lie down flat on the ground and then piled bricks on his tummy, higher and higher. Poor Twiddle woke up suddenly, and wondered what the heavy weight was on the top of him.

The cat of course! It had jumped in at the bedroom window, meaning to go downstairs and find its basket. But the bedroom door was shut and it couldn't. So it had jumped up on to Twiddle and settled down there, warm and comfortable.

"Well, that's the last straw!" said Twiddle, in a rage, heaving the cat off the bed. "To-morrow I sell you. Yes, I do. I sell you. So make up your mind to it, Cat — you're going to be sold."

Twiddle meant what he said. The cat managed to trip him up twice the next day, and then Twiddle caught her, and put her into a box. He shut down the lid, tied it with string and set off.

He walked about two miles and came to a small cottage where there lived an old woman who was very fond of cats. She had once been to tea with Mrs. Twiddle, and had taken such a fancy to the cat that she had offered to buy it. But Mrs. Twiddle wouldn't sell it.

It didn't take Twiddle long to sell the cat to the old woman. He got twenty-five new pence for her, and was very pleased. He thought he would spend the money on beautiful roses to put in Mrs. Twiddle's bedroom. So he stopped at the flower-shop and bought a pretty bunch of red and pink ones.

When he got home he found a telegram from Mrs. Twiddle. "Amanda is better. Returning home this afternoon."

"Good," thought Mr. Twiddle, pleased. He set to work to clean the house and make it nice for Mrs. Twiddle. He went out and bought a meat pie and some tarts. He put the roses into water, and they made the bedroom smell beautiful.

Mrs. Twiddle came home and was pleased to see everything looking so nice, and she simply *loved* the roses. "Oh, how beautiful!" she cried. "How kind of you, Twiddle dear. But where *did* you get the money from? They must have cost quite a lot of money."

Twiddle suddenly felt that he didn't want to explain about selling the cat. He cleared his throat, smiled rather nervously, and stared at Mrs. Twiddle.

"I might have sold the cat, mightn't I?" he said, with a queer little laugh.

"Of course, you wouldn't do a thing like that!" said Mrs. Twiddle. "What, be so cruel and unkind as to sell my dear, darling old puss-cat that I love? Don't be silly, Twiddle. You know if you did a thing like that I'd chase you out of the house with my umbrella, and not let you in again till you brought the cat back."

This was very alarming. Twiddle had had no idea that Mrs. Twiddle would feel like this about the cat. He went very red and felt frightened.

"But I'm sure you haven't sold the cat. You've bought me some lovely, lovely

roses out of your own money," said Mrs. Twiddle, and she gave poor Mr. Twiddle a big kiss. "And now where is puss? I thought she'd be here to greet me."

Twiddle began to tremble, thinking that surely he would be chased out of the house with an umbrella in a minute or two. And then a most surprising thing happened.

The cat ran in at the door, went straight to Mrs. Twiddle, rubbed against her skirt, and made some very loving noises.

"You darling. You came to greet me, after all. Where were you? Did you know that Twiddle said he might have sold you! Isn't he a naughty story-teller?"

Twiddle was very thankful to see the cat, but dear, dear, how was he going to make it up to the old woman who had bought her. The cat must have run away from her and come all the way home. She would be sure to come and call and ask if the cat had come back.

"There's only one thing to be done," thought Twiddle gloomily. "I must empty my pockets, and see if I have enough money. I must take it to her and say the cat is back. Then perhaps Mrs. Twiddle will never know how foolish I have been."

So poor Twiddle took back most of his pocket-money to the old woman who had bought the cat.

He couldn't buy any tobacco, sweets or papers for a week. Poor Twiddle. I don't suppose he'll ever really like the cat now, do you?

CHAPTER X

MRS. TWIDDLE'S NECKLACE

Mrs. Twiddle had a sister called Julia, and one day, on Mrs. Twiddle's birthday, Julia sent her a bead necklace.

Mrs. Twiddle was delighted with it. She showed it proudly to Twiddle.

"Look, Twiddle," she said. "Did you ever see such dear little beads? All different colours, and all sizes and shapes! Julia must have threaded this pretty necklace herself. She always was a clever one with her hands."

"Very nice, dear, very nice indeed," said Twiddle. "It will look beautiful with the new dress I have given you."

It did. It went with it very nicely, and Mrs. Twiddle enjoyed going out to tea in her new dress, wearing the string of tiny, coloured beads round her neck. She was really very proud of her new necklace, and liked it very much.

One day, just as she was going out

shopping, the necklace broke! Mrs. Twiddle was dreadfully upset. Some of the beads were left on the string but most of them went tumbling and bouncing all over the floor.

"Oh, look at that now!" said Mrs. Twiddle in dismay. "Twiddle, come and pick them up for me, quick! I can't stop, or I shall miss the bus."

"Certainly, love, certainly," said Twiddle,

folding up his newspaper carefully and getting out of his chair. "Dear, dear, what a pity! But don't you worry now—I'll find every one of the beads, and you can take them to the jeweller's and get them properly re-threaded."

"Twiddle, be sure you put them somewhere safe when you've found them all," said Mrs. Twiddle, putting on her hat. "Now don't you put them somewhere silly, where I shall never find them. Put them in the little jug on the dresser. That would be a good place for them."

"All right, dear," said Twiddle, busy hunting for the beads on the floor. "Goodbye. Don't miss the bus. I'll have all the beads found and put away safely by the time you come back."

Mrs. Twiddle hurried off to catch her bus. Twiddle went on looking for the beads. It was astonishing how far they had bounded and rolled.

The cat came strolling in as he was hunting for them, and was astonished, but pleased, to find Twiddle on all-fours on the floor. She had an idea he meant to play with her, so she playfully leapt at him, knocking about twenty beads out of his hand as she did so.

"Just the sort of silly thing you *would* do!" said Twiddle, staring at the cat in disgust. "Go away. I never knew such a cat for coming in when it wasn't wanted. Go and catch mice!"

The cat understood the word "mice" and ran about excitedly looking for one,

getting into Twiddle's way in a most annoying manner. Every time he put his hand under the sofa or chair to get a bead the cat put out her paw and patted him, so that he kept dropping the bead.

"Go away!" he said to the cat. "Who can pick up beads with you bothering round like this? My gracious, what a lot there are all over the place. I shall never find them all with you gambolling round."

The cat felt that Twiddle was not really pleased with her company, and she strolled out, tail in air. Twiddle was glad. Now he could find the beads quickly, put them away, and sit down to read his paper.

He found all he could, and stood up with them safe in his hand. Now, where did Mrs. Twiddle tell him he could put them?

"Ah — in that jug on the dresser, of course," said Twiddle. He went to the dresser, reached up, and popped all the beads into the jug. But they didn't make the little rattling noise he expected to hear. So he reached down the jug and looked into it.

It was half-full of milk! Bother! Now he would have to empty the milk into the flat plate and scrape out all the beads and dry them. Mrs. Twiddle wouldn't be at all pleased to see them swimming in the milk.

So Twiddle poured the milk into a flat enamel plate and then went to get a spoon to scrape out the beads.

The cat came in whilst he was getting the spoon, and saw the milk in the plate. How nice of Twiddle to set out so much milk for her, she thought. She jumped up on the table and began lapping it.

Twiddle heard her, and was angry. He shooed her away. "You again! Always interfering! I suppose you've swallowed half the beads!"

The cat thought that Twiddle was most unreasonable that afternoon. She went to the window-sill, sat down in the sun, and began to wash herself slowly and thoroughly, watching Twiddle out of one of her bright green eyes as she did so.

"Stare all you like, silly animal," said Twiddle, who was not fond of the cat. "It's not my fault the beads went into the milk. It's Mrs. Twiddle's. She should have remembered there was milk in the jug."

Twiddle got all the beads out and carefully dried them. He emptied the milk back again into the jug, spilling quite a lot on the floor as he did so.

"You can lick that up," he told the cat. "It will save me getting a cloth to wipe up the mess."

But the cat had had enough of Twiddle that afternoon. She felt quite certain that as soon as she leapt down to lap up the spilt milk Twiddle would send her away again. So she took no notice and went on washing herself.

"You really are a most annoying and disobedient cat," said Twiddle. "Most disobliging. Now I've got to wipe up the mess myself."

When he had wiped it up he stared at the little pile of beads. What should he do with them? Where would a safe place be?

He looked at the dresser. What about putting them in another jug? But there was

114

no jug there. They were all in the larder.

"Well, what about the teapot? That's an even better place," thought Twiddle, and he took it down from the shelf.

He put the beads into it, then put on the lid. "There now! They are perfectly safe. Isn't that good?"

He took up his newspaper, sat down in his chair, and began to read. He had a very peaceful time till Mrs. Twiddle came back.

She brought her sister Julia with her.

"Hallo, Twiddle dear," said Mrs. Twiddle. "Wasn't it lucky, I met Julia and told her I'd broken my necklace, and she said she'd come back and have tea with us and thread the beads again herself. Now, wasn't that kind of her?"

"Oh, very," said Twiddle. "Very kind indeed. Shall I put the kettle on to boil, wife?"

"No, I'll do that," said Mrs. Twiddle, who knew that Twiddle would probably put the kettle on and forget to light the gas. "You show Julia the beads and get out my work-basket so that she can get the needle and thread ready to mend the necklace after tea."

Twiddle gave Julia the work-basket, and then looked round for the beads. Where had he put them?

"The beads, Twiddle," said Julia. "Where are they?"

"What did you do with them?" asked Mrs. Twiddle. "Did you put them into that jug?"

"Oh, yes, I did," said Twiddle. "But wait a minute—the jug had milk in it so I had to take out the beads after all. It was such a business."

"Well, where did you put the beads after that?" said Mrs. Twiddle, impatiently.

The cat looked at Twiddle as if it could tell him. Twiddle looked at the cat. But he simply could not remember where he had put those beads! He felt in his pockets. He looked in the little jar on the mantelpiece where odds-and-ends were often put. He opened the desk and looked there.

"Oh, Twiddle, for goodness' sake stop fiddling about and find the beads!" said Julia. "You *must* know where you put them!"

The cat knew, but Twiddle still didn't. He really had a very bad memory indeed.

"Oh, let's have tea and perhaps Twiddle will remember by that time," said Julia.

"Here's the teapot," said Twiddle, anxious to help. He took the teapot to the stove, and stood it there to warm it.

Mrs. Twiddle took off the lid and popped

in four spoonfuls of tea. Then she poured the boiling water in.

"Nice hot cup of tea!" she said. "It will do us all good."

They sat down to tea. There was bread-and-butter and jam, and some nice new chocolate buns. Twiddle felt that he was really going to enjoy his tea.

"Sugar and milk, Julia?" asked Mrs. Twiddle, and put them both into Julia's cup. Then she poured out the tea, and Twiddle handed the cup to Julia.

Then Mrs. Twiddle poured out Twiddle a cup of tea and then one for herself. The beads came rushing out of the spout with the tea, and settled down at the bottom of each cup.

Everyone took sugar so they had to stir their tea. Twiddle stirred his sharply, and then gazed at it in astonishment. All kinds of little round coloured things surged round and round the surface as he stirred it.

"What are they?" thought Twiddle. "Bubbles?"

Julia also stirred her tea and looked down at it in surprise. As for Mrs. Twiddle, she was really alarmed.

"Don't drink the tea!" she cried. "There's something wrong with it—insects or something! Goodness gracious, how disgusting!"

Twiddle stared down at his cup—and an awful thought came into his head. Beads! He had put the beads into the teapot for

safety! And he had forgotten. So Mrs. Twiddle had made tea out of tea-leaves, hot water — and beads! Now what would she say?

Mrs. Twiddle got some of the beads into her spoon and stared at them in astonishment and anger.

"My *beads*!" she said. "Why, they're my *beads*!"

"Well — just fancy that — so they are!" said Twiddle.

"How *did* they get into the tea?" said Julia, in surprise. "Are there any in the teapot, dear?"

Whilst Mrs. Twiddle was looking, Twiddle got up very quickly and left the room. He went into the garden and sat down in the woodshed. He felt that he knew everything that Mrs. Twiddle and Julia would say. He really didn't want to hear it. It was a pity to miss his tea, but the wood-shed would be much more peaceful than the kitchen.

The cat walked in and stared at Twiddle. It made him angry. "You go away!" said

Twiddle. "Just come to gloat over me, haven't you? Well, you go and tell Mrs. Twiddle and Julia that they're always making a fuss about nothing and I'm NOT GOING TO STAND IT. See?"

But the cat wasn't bold enough to say anything like that to Mrs. Twiddle! No— it just sat there waiting for Mrs. Twiddle to come and fetch Mr. Twiddle in. It knew there would be some fun then!

CHAPTER XI

MR. TWIDDLE AND THE TICKETS

Mr. and Mrs. Twiddle were going away for a holiday. What fun!

"Now I'll do all the packing," said Mrs. Twiddle. "If you do it you'll take the most ridiculous things and leave out all the ones we shall really want."

"No, I shan't," said Twiddle, feeling hurt.

"Well, don't you remember last time you did the packing?" said Mrs. Twiddle. "You packed the kitchen poker and although it was summer-time, you packed all your winter vests. I never did know why you packed the poker."

"Only because I thought it might come in useful," said Mr. Twiddle. "You never know when or where you might meet a burglar."

"Well—I'll do the packing this time," said Mrs. Twiddle, "and then we shall be certain of our tooth-brushes and nightclothes and hankies and things like that. I'll ask Julia, my sister, if she'll have the cat whilst we're away."

"I'm glad we're not going to pack the cat, anyway," said Twiddle, who thought their cat was a most interfering nuisance. He was always falling over her.

"And I'll shut up the house and tell the milkman not to leave any milk," went on Mrs. Twiddle.

"It seems to me as if you're going to do everything and leave me nothing to do at all," said Mr. Twiddle. "Can't I do *any*thing?"

"Yes — you can go and buy the railway tickets," said Mrs. Twiddle. "And mind you put them somewhere safe so that you don't lose them."

So Twiddle went to buy the tickets. He put them into his pocket — nice green tickets that would take him and Mrs. Twiddle to the seaside for a lovely holiday. Mr. Twiddle inquired about the trains.

"There's one at ten o'clock and one at eleven," said the porter. "You had better be here ten minutes before the train goes, with your luggage, then I can get you good corner seats."

"Right," said Twiddle. "Thank you very much."

He went home. "I've got the tickets, wife," he said, and he showed her them. "So we shan't have to get them on the day. That will save us a minute or two."

"Where are you going to put them?"

asked Mrs. Twiddle. "Don't put them into the teapot, please, where you once put my beads. I couldn't bear to drink ticket-tea."

"Of course I shan't do a thing like that," said Twiddle, crossly. "I shall put them somewhere very safe indeed."

"Well, for goodness' sake tell me where you are going to put them," said Mrs. Twiddle, "because you are sure to forget, and I shall have to remind you."

Twiddle looked round the kitchen. Should he put them into the picture-frame.

"No," he thought. "Mrs. Twiddle might go dusting there and flick them out."

He looked round again. Should he put them inside the clock? He wound the clock up every night, and he could see them there each time, and be reminded where they were.

"No. That won't do either," he thought. "Mrs. Twiddle is always talking of sending the clock to be mended. It would be awful if she did send it, and the tickets, too. Dear me, where *can* I put them?"

Then he thought he would put them into

his hatband. They would be safe there because his hat-band was very tight, and he would see them every time he went out. He went to put them there, but then he changed his mind.

"No. It might rain when I was out, then the tickets would get wet and soft," he thought. "Oh, dear—where can I put these silly railway tickets? I wish I hadn't gone and got them."

Well, in the end, Twiddle decided that the very safest place of all would be in his waistcoat pocket! Then he would be bound to take them to the station with him, because he would be wearing his waistcoat, anyhow!

"Have you found a place for the tickets, Twiddle?" asked Mrs. Twiddle, at last. Twiddle nodded.

"Yes," he said. "A very sensible place, too. In my waistcoat pocket."

"Good," said Mrs. Twiddle. "You simply can't help taking them with you if you put them there."

Mrs. Twiddle soon started her packing

and finished it. She got Twiddle to sit on the trunk whilst she strapped it up. She went to her sister Julia with the cat. But when she got home again the cat was there before her. It didn't like Julia.

"It's a very silly cat, the way it behaves," said Twiddle, in disgust. "It's not a bit of good you taking it to Julia. It will keep on and on coming back. Can't it catch mice and rats for itself? It always seems to me to look after itself very well."

But Mrs. Twiddle didn't like the idea of leaving the cat without anyone to see to it. So once more she took it round to Julia, and this time it was locked into the scullery, and was not able to get home before Mrs. Twiddle did.

The great morning came. Mr. and Mrs. Twiddle had an early breakfast, shut up the house, and got into the taxi-cab that called for them.

On the way to the station Mrs. Twiddle asked Twiddle to get the tickets ready. He felt round for them.

But what was this—he hadn't got his waistcoat on! He was wearing his pullover instead! Mrs. Twiddle stared at Twiddle in dismay.

"You stupid man! You decided to wear your pullover instead of your waistcoat— and now you must have gone and left the tickets behind. Quick—tell the taxi-man to go back."

Twiddle rapped on the window and told the man to turn and go back. He felt very cross with himself. They got to the house and Twiddle jumped out. He unlocked the front door and went in. He ran up the stairs and went to the wardrobe.

His waistcoat was there. Twiddle ran his fingers into the pockets and gave a loud groan. There were no tickets there!

"My, my, my!" said Twiddle. "What

have I done with them? Now I come to think of it I did take them out when I took off the waistcoat and decided to put on my pullover! But where did I put them?"

He felt in all his pockets. He looked in his hat-band. He looked in his shoes!

No tickets. He heard Mrs. Twiddle calling out to him. "Twiddle, Twiddle! What in the world are you doing? Do you want to miss the train? For goodness' sake come along."

"Coming, coming!" yelled Mr. Twiddle, and hurriedly looked all round the bedroom for the tickets. He looked in the drawers. No tickets. He looked on the washstand. No tickets. He looked under the bed. Certainly no tickets.

"TWIDDLE! It's ten to ten. You MUST come!" called Mrs. Twiddle, and the taximan hooted his horn so loudly that all the neighbours looked out of their windows in surprise.

"JUST coming!" yelled poor Twiddle, and went down the stairs three steps at a time. He ran into the kitchen. He must have put the tickets there.

He looked inside the clock. No tickets. He looked in the picture-frame. No tickets. He even looked inside the teapot, the milk-jug and the sugar-basin. But there were no tickets to be seen anywhere.

Mrs. Twiddle got out of the cab and came hastily into the house. "Twiddle! What are you doing? Why don't you come? We shall certainly miss the train."

"I can't find the tickets," said poor Twiddle, his face as red as a beetroot.

"Toot-toot-toot!" went the taxi-man's horn.

Mrs. Twiddle made a clicking noise that Twiddle hated, because it always meant that she felt very cross.

"I might have guessed it!" she said. "The one thing I asked you to do! Was there ever a sillier man than you? Well, well—you have probably put them down the sink, or in the dustbin, or even on the rubbish-heap, so it's no good looking for them. Come along. We shall have to buy some more."

Mr. Twiddle slammed the front door. He

went out to the taxi-cab, and as he went he saw something lying on the garden wall. It was the cat.

"Look at that," he said to Mrs. Twiddle. "There's the cat back again. I hope you won't take her to Julia again."

"Oh dear," said Mrs. Twiddle, in dismay. "No, we haven't time. She must go with us! I am sure she would sit quietly on your knee all the time."

"What! Take that cat with us — on my knee!" cried Twiddle, horrified. "You know it doesn't like me. Why, part of the niceness of having a holiday was leaving that cat behind. It's always interfering with me."

"Well, Puss will have to come," said Mrs. Twiddle firmly. "Hold your tongue, Twiddle. What with losing the tickets, *and* losing the train, you've done enough for one morning."

The train could be heard whistling in the distance. It had come into the station and was now whistling its way out. How tiresome! Now they had missed it.

"Train's gone, ma'am," said the taxi-driver.

"I know," said Mrs. Twiddle. "Twiddle, take the cat, please. I've got the lunch-basket to carry."

"I'll carry the basket," said Twiddle. "You carry the cat."

"No. You'd lose the lunch-things," said

Mrs. Twiddle. "Here's the cat. You can't lose *her* — she'll be frightened and stick close to you."

They arrived at the station. "I must go and buy some new tickets," said Mrs. Twiddle. "Now, hold on to the cat and stand just here, so that I know where you are."

Mrs. Twiddle went to the ticket-office. She opened her bag to get out her money — and there, neatly tucked in among the coins were two green railway tickets! Mrs. Twiddle stared at them.

"The tickets!" she said. "They're in my bag! How in the world did they get there?"

She hurried back to Twiddle, who was trying to stop the cat from putting her claws into his shoulder.

"Twiddle! Look here! How did these tickets get into my bag?"

Twiddle stared — and then he grinned in delight.

"Of course! That is where I put them when I changed my waistcoat for a pull-over! I remember thinking that the very safest place of all would be your bag, because you are never parted from that, and you would be sure to take it to the station with you. Wasn't I clever, wife?"

"It would have been cleverer to remember where you had put them," said Mrs. Twiddle. "We have missed the train. But never mind—the porter says there is another at eleven o'clock, and it's faster than the one we missed and won't be so

crowded. And anyway it was a good thing we had to go back, because we found poor old Puss, and she'll be able to have a holiday with us."

"Oh my!" groaned Twiddle to himself. "Why didn't I remember I'd popped the tickets into Mrs. Twiddle's bag? Then we wouldn't have gone back and found the cat. Now she'll spoil my holiday, I know she will! In future I'll be sensible and remember every single thing!"

But he won't, will he! Poor old Twiddle. He had the cat on his knee all the way to the seaside, and dear me, how she did dig her twenty claws into him!

CHAPTER XII

MR. TWIDDLE'S MEAT PIE

"My sister Harriet has asked us to go and see her tomorrow, Twiddle dear," said Mrs. Twiddle. "Won't that be nice?"

Twiddle didn't think it would be at all nice. He didn't like Harriet. She was always remembering silly things he had done, and reminding him of them. It wouldn't be so bad if Harriet did silly things herself, then he could do some remembering, too. But she never did anything silly.

"Well," said Twiddle, "well—do you think we ought to go when food is so expensive? We shall have to have dinner there, you know."

"How nice of you to think of such a thing," said Mrs. Twiddle, pleased. "Quite right—food is expensive just now—so you can go out this afternoon and buy a meat pie from the cookie-shop. You won't have to stand in the queue for more than an hour, I should think."

Twiddle wished he hadn't said anything about food or dinner. Now he would have to take a basket, go out in the rain and hope the meat pies wouldn't be all sold by the time he got his turn.

But he had to go. "Put on your mack and your goloshes," said Mrs. Twiddle. "And take an umbrella. And remember to put it up, Twiddle. Last time you went out in the rain with your umbrella you forgot to put it up."

"All right, all right," said Twiddle. He put on his mack and his goloshes, took his umbrella and a basket, and out he walked. He didn't have to stand very long in the queue after all, and he got a fine big meat pie, piping hot and smelling most delicious. He felt quite pleased with himself.

When he got home, Mrs. Twiddle, who was upstairs, shouted down to him: "Stand your umbrella in the porch outside to dry. Put your goloshes in the boot-cupboard, and put the meat pie in the larder."

Well, Mr. Twiddle put all the things away, but, unfortunately, he made a little

mistake. He stood his umbrella in the porch outside all right, but he was rather dreamy when he took his goloshes off, and he put them on the shelf in the larder instead of in the boot-cupboard.

Then he put the meat pie into the boot-cupboard and shut the door. He whistled a little tune, went into the kitchen, sat down and took up the newspaper. Now, perhaps he could have a little rest.

Mrs. Twiddle hurried down, poked the

fire, found her knitting, and sat down, too. She chattered away to Twiddle, who said, "Ooom, ooom," now and then, and went on reading his newspaper.

The cat came into the kitchen and mewed.

"What do you want, Pussy?" said Mrs. Twiddle. "Do you want a drink? Twiddle, give the cat some milk."

"It doesn't want a drink," said Twiddle, who hated to be disturbed by the cat. "It's just mewing. It doesn't want a drink every time it mews."

"Give it some milk, Twiddle," said Mrs. Twiddle; and Mr. Twiddle did. The cat drank it. It went out into the hall and smelt round about the boot-cupboard. It came back and mewed again. It could smell the pie in the cupboard, and it felt astonished and excited.

"See if the cat wants to go out-of-doors, Twiddle," said Mrs. Twiddle.

"It doesn't," said Twiddle. "It's just being a nuisance. Go away, Puss. I want to read my paper."

"Let the cat out, Twiddle," said Mrs. Twiddle; and Mr. Twiddle did. But it came in again almost at once, jumping through the window very near to Twiddle's head. It made him jump, and he was annoyed with the cat.

"Can't you make up your mind what you want?" he said to it, fiercely. "You don't seem to know if you're coming or going. Sit down and wash yourself."

The cat didn't. It gave Twiddle a rude stare, then went into the hall again. It smelt round the boot-cupboard, feeling more and more excited. Either there was a boot there that smelt exactly like a meat pie or, by some surprising chance, there really *was* a pie inside. The cat couldn't open the cupboard, but it tried to, scraping away at the edge with its claws.

Mrs. Twiddle heard it. She wondered what the cat wanted. Perhaps there was a mouse in the hall. "Twiddle," she said, "see what the cat wants, will you? It's making such a noise out there."

"It doesn't want anything," said Twiddle,

annoyed. "It's just being tiresome. It often is."

"Go and see what the cat wants," said Mrs. Twiddle; and Twiddle went. He watched the cat nosing round the boot-cupboard. He saw a fine way of getting rid of the cat for the whole afternoon. He'd shut it in the boot-cupboard and let it sniff round for mice there and be happy.

So Mr. Twiddle opened the cupboard door, shot the cat in quickly, and closed the door again. Then he went back to his chair and took up his newspaper.

The cat soon found the pie. It was still in its paper bag, so it had to tear the paper open. It pulled the pie around among the boots, and had a glorious time. Mrs. Twiddle was surprised to hear it making such a noise in the cupboard.

"What *can* the cat be doing?" she said.

"Ooom?" said Mr. Twiddle, not taking any notice.

"It seems to be tearing paper," said Mrs. Twiddle.

"Let it," said Twiddle, annoyed.

The cat lost a bit of pie down a boot and scrabbled after it. "Good gracious, you haven't shut the poor cat in the boot-cupboard, have you?" said Mrs. Twiddle.

"Hunting for mice, I expect," said Twiddle, feeling that at any moment he would have to get up again and let the cat out.

"That reminds me," said Mrs. Twiddle. "What sort of meat pie did you get? Was it

nice and fresh? Was it a nice big one?"

"A beauty," said Twiddle.

"I think I'll have a look at it," said Mrs. Twiddle. "If it's on the small side we'd better take a pound of sausages with us, too."

"I tell you it's a nice big one," said Twiddle, in alarm, thinking that he would now be told to go out and buy sausages. Mrs. Twiddle got up and went to the larder. She opened the door—and the very first thing she saw was a pair of dirty goloshes standing on the shelf. She gave a squeal.

"Gracious! What's this?"

"What's what?" said Twiddle.

"*This!*" said Mrs. Twiddle, indignantly, and she held up the goloshes. "On my clean shelf, in my clean larder! What do you mean by it, Twiddle? Have you gone mad?"

Twiddle stared at the goloshes. He must have put them there without thinking. "Er—er—sorry, wife," he said. "It was a mistake."

"I should think it was," said Mrs. Twiddle,

throwing the goloshes on to the floor. "Now, where's that meat pie? *I* can't see it!"

No meat pie was there. Mrs. Twiddle turned to Twiddle and scolded him. "Where did you put the pie? Didn't I tell you to put it here? Have you taken it to your bedroom? Have you left it in the porch?"

Mr. Twiddle couldn't remember. "I'll

go and look," he said. Mrs. Twiddle pointed to his goloshes.

"Put them into the boot-cupboard as you go by," she said. Twiddle picked them up. He went to the boot-cupboard and opened it. The cat shot out at once, looking remarkably fat. A curious smell came from the cupboard — rather tasty and rich. Mr. Twiddle smelt it — and a peculiar look came over his face.

He must have put the meat pie into the boot-cupboard instead of his goloshes. And he had shut the cat in there too — so there wouldn't be any meat pie left. It was all very tiresome. What could he do about it?

"Have you found that meat pie yet?" called Mrs. Twiddle. "I can't see it anywhere."

"Well, dear," said Mr. Twiddle, going into the kitchen, trying to smile, "well, dear, it's like this — you see — well, what I did was — er, er . . . it's very funny really."

Mrs. Twiddle looked at him and a cold stare came over her face. "What have you done now, Twiddle?" she said. "*Don't* tell me you put the meat pie into the boot-cupboard—and shut the cat in there too!"

"Well—I won't tell you if you'd rather I didn't," said Twiddle, backing out of the kitchen. "But I must have done something like that—quite by mistake, of course—and how was I to know the cat was smelling it? Well, I'll go out and get another."

He went out—but he didn't get another, because they were all sold out. Mrs. Twiddle was cross.

"Now we shan't be able to go and see Harriet," she said. "I'm not going unless I take something with me—and they don't make pies to-morrow. We can't go. What a pity!"

"Well!" thought Twiddle, sitting down in his chair and picking up his paper again, "that's a bit of good luck anyway! Shan't see Harriet to-morrow after all. That *is* a bit of good luck. And it looks as if I'll be able to read my paper in peace now."

The cat came into the kitchen, mewing. "Poor creature!" said Mrs. Twiddle. "All that meat pie has made it feel ill. Nurse it a bit, Twiddle. I've got to get the tea. But mind it isn't ill all over you."

The cat jumped up on Twiddle's knee. He looked at her with disgust—always going in and out and jumping up and down —never still for a moment. As soon as Mrs. Twiddle went out of the room he pushed her off, and flapped her away with his paper.

"Ssssss!" he hissed at her. "Go away. I'll shut you into the boot-cupboard again, if you're not careful—with*out* a meat pie this time! Sssssssss!"

CHAPTER XIII

MR. TWIDDLE AND THE SNOW

It was a very snowy day. Mr. Twiddle hoped that Mrs. Twiddle wouldn't want him to go out in it. It was difficult to walk in thick snow, and Mr. Twiddle felt he would much rather sit by the fire and read the paper.

But soon he heard Mrs. Twiddle's voice. "I hope you are not going to sit indoors this fine day, Twiddle. The sun is out now. It will do you good to go out. Will you fetch me some fish from the fishmonger's?"

Twiddle groaned. He knew he would have to. He put on his goloshes and his coat and hat, took a basket and set out. The children were having a fine time that day. They were making snowballs and throwing them, they were building snowmen, and they were sliding down the big hill nearby on sledges.

Mr. Twiddle had quite a time dodging snowballs and sledges. Then he stood still and watched some children at the top of the hill, making a very big snowball indeed.

"We're going to roll it down the hill and it will get bigger and bigger," they cried. Mr. Twiddle watched as they began to roll the big ball downwards.

Half-way down it was very big indeed. Then it began to roll down by itself, like a round avalanche. It came down more and more quickly, and Twiddle tried to hop out of the way. But he was just too late and the great big snowball struck him very hard indeed.

Mr. Twiddle was knocked right over. Then he was taken onwards with the snowball, which was still rolling and gathering more snow. On and on he went, rolling over and over, getting the snow all round him. Then the snowball stopped, in the middle of the village street, which just then happened to be empty.

"Didn't it roll well!" shouted the children on the hill. "Let's make another."

They hadn't seen that their snowball had knocked down and taken Mr. Twiddle along with it. They set to work to make another.

Mr. Twiddle was buried in the middle of the big snowball. He didn't like it. He had snow down his neck, and in his mouth, ears, and nose. It was cold and horrid. Mr. Twiddle began to struggle and groan.

An old lady came by and she looked in alarm at the snowball. What peculiar noises were coming out of it! What was the matter with it?

"Grrrrrrrrr," said Twiddle, growling with anger in the middle of the snowball, trying to get his head out. A little dog came up and barked in excitement.

The old lady hurried off to tell a policeman. "There's a snowball behaving in a very strange manner," she told him. "Right in the middle of the village street. It said 'Grrrrrrr' just like a dog."

"I'll see into the matter," said the policeman, looking surprised. He went off to the snowball and looked at it. What a big one! And what noises came from it. He scratched his head and wondered if he ought to arrest a snowball.

Presently some more people came up and looked at the snowball, which was now wriggling a bit here and there, and was still making strange noises.

"What is it?" said everyone. "Is there some animal inside? Who put the snowball here?"

Suddenly out shot Mr. Twiddle's head, and he blinked round at everyone in surprise. The policeman jumped and stared. Why, this must be some sort of a snowman! He took out his notebook.

"How did you get into the snow? Are you pretending to be a snowman? Did you build the snow up all round yourself?" cried the people, in surprise.

"Help me out," said Mr. Twiddle. "I've lost my glasses in the snow."

"I'll have to arrest you for obstructing the traffic," said the policeman, and wrote in his notebook.

"How can I obstruct traffic when there isn't any?" said Twiddle, indignantly, trying to get his arms out of the snowball.

"Well, you would have obstructed it if there had been any," said the policeman. "You come along-a me."

"How can I? I'm in the middle of this big snowball," said Twiddle. "Do you suppose I like being here? Nobody helps me at all!"

"Well, you got yourself in, so I suppose you can get yourself out," said the policeman.

"When I get out I'm going to tell you a

few things," said Twiddle, angrily, "and I shouldn't be a bit surprised to find myself pulling your nose!"

"Now, now, look here, you can't talk to the police like that!" said the policeman, crossly. "As soon as you're out of that snowball I'm going to take you straight to the police-station!"

That made Twiddle feel upset. He didn't want to be marched off to the police-station. What would Mrs. Twiddle say if she heard he was locked up? He would never hear the last of it.

He stopped trying to get out of the big snowball. Perhaps if he stayed there quietly the policeman would get tired of waiting and would go away. But he didn't. He began to scrape at the snow to free Twiddle. He badly wanted to take him off to the police-station now. He would show Twiddle that he couldn't talk about pulling noses!

Goodness knows what would have happened if the children at the top of the hill hadn't sent down another enormous snowball! It came bounding down the hill,

getting bigger and bigger as it came. It shot
into the village street, and arrived at top
speed just where the crowd stood, watching
Twiddle.

In a trice everyone was bowled over, and
buried in the snow, for the snowball burst
all over them. The policeman was right
underneath. He lost his helmet, his notebook, and his temper.

As soon as Twiddle saw everyone on the ground, groping about wildly, he saw his chance of escape. He struck out at the snow surrounding him, managed to get free, found his glasses, and rushed off home. He didn't stop till he got there. Then he put on his glasses, brushed down his coat, and went indoors.

"Well," he thought, as he sat down in his chair and picked up the paper, "well— I'm not going out again to-day for anyone in the world! What a time I've had! Nearly buried in snow—almost taken off to prison . . . well, well, well."

"Is that you, Twiddle?" called Mrs. Twiddle. "Put the fish in the larder, will you?"

Twiddle frowned and rubbed his nose. He had forgotten all about the fish! Now what was he to do? Well, he wouldn't say anything at all, and perhaps Mrs. Twiddle wouldn't notice the fish wasn't there, till the next day when she wanted to cook it.

But she did notice it. She went to the larder to cut a bit off the fish for the cat—

and to her surprise there was no fish there!

"Twiddle! There's no fish! The cat must have had it! How many times have I told you not to leave the larder door open?"

"About six hundred times," said Twiddle, politely.

"Don't be rude," said Mrs. Twiddle. "Well, what a waste—to think all that fish is inside the cat. Go and put on your hat and coat and fetch some more."

Twiddle groaned. He went to fetch his hat and coat and then Mrs. Twiddle appeared too, dressed ready to go out. "It's such a nice afternoon," she said. "I thought I would come with you."

"Well, if you're going out, I may as well stay at home," said Twiddle, pleased, and took off his hat. But no, he had to go, to keep Mrs. Twiddle company.

On the way they met the policeman, who had a black eye because someone had kicked him by accident when they had all been knocked over by the snowball. Mrs. Twiddle was very sorry to see it.

"Ah," said the policeman, stroking his eye gently. "Ah, I had a bad time this morning. I was just about to make an arrest of a man who was obstructing the traffic and being very rude to me, when a big snowball knocked me down, and my prisoner escaped."

"What bad luck!" said Mrs. Twiddle. "Fancy the man being rude to you! I wonder that he dared to."

"He said he would pull my nose," said

the policeman. Mrs. Twiddle clicked her tongue in horror, and then walked on with Twiddle, who hadn't said a word all the time.

"Would you believe it!" said Mrs. Twiddle, in a tone of horror. "Well, Twiddle, silly though you are sometimes, I'm quite sure *you* would never be rude to a policeman."

And still Twiddle never said a word. Well, there wasn't anything he could say! Poor Twiddle.

CHAPTER XIV

MR. TWIDDLE ISN'T VERY HELPFUL

Mr. Twiddle was out shopping. He had a list of things to buy, which Mrs. Twiddle had written out for him. She said he would never remember any of them if she didn't, and she was quite right, he would not remember.

"I've got a visitor coming," she said to Mr. Twiddle. "A brother of my best friend. So be sure you bring everything back with you, Twiddle, and I can give him a nice lunch."

Twiddle went to the grocer's. By him was a dear old lady, and on the floor beside her was a shopping bag, quite full. Next to her was a big burly fellow, buying all kinds of things.

The old lady was served and she went out of the shop. It was Twiddle's turn next, and he began to read from his list. "Half a pound of bacon. One pound of sugar. A pot of strawberry jam."

And then Twiddle saw on the floor, near him the shopping bag, quite full! He stared at it. Why, that dear old lady must have gone off without her bag! How upset she would be.

"Excuse me a minute," said Twiddle to the surprised shop-girl. He snatched up the bag, and hurried out of the shop, leaving his list on the counter till he came back.

"I must catch up that dear old lady!" he

thought. "I really must. Poor old thing—how very worried she will be when she finds she hasn't got her shopping!"

The old lady was right away in the distance. "She walks fast," thought Twiddle, and set off after her. He almost ran, because he was so anxious to catch her up.

He hadn't gone very far before he heard a shout behind him. He turned round and saw the shop-girl and the big, burly man both yelling and waving to him. "Oh dear—I suppose they're telling me they have found my shopping list and want me to go back for it!" thought Mr. Twiddle. He stood still and shouted back.

"I'll be back in a minute!" Then on he went again, running to catch up the old lady.

The big, burly man set out after Mr. Twiddle. "Hi!" he yelled. "You come back! Hi!"

Mr. Twiddle thought the man was foolish. He might guess he would be coming back soon! So he took no notice and hurried on. The man hurried, too.

"You wait till I catch you!" yelled the man. "You just wait!"

Twiddle thought that was a bit queer. Why should he be caught? What did the man mean? He must be a little mad.

Twiddle went faster, taking a look now and again over his shoulder. The man looked hot and angry.

"I'll shake you till your teeth rattle!" yelled the man. "I'll pull your ears! I'll . . ."

Twiddle felt really alarmed. Why was this man so annoyed? He really must be quite mad. Twiddle ran so fast that he panted like an engine going uphill.

Suddenly he felt a heavy hand on his shoulder, and he was pulled to a stop. The big, burly man swung little Mr. Twiddle round and glared at him.

"Hand over that bag!" he said, angrily.

"Certainly not," said Twiddle. "It's not yours. This is robbery!"

"It certainly is—but *you're* the robber!" said the man, very red in the face. "Give me that bag."

"I shall not," said Twiddle. "It belongs

163

to that dear old lady just down the road there."

"Oh, you naughty story-teller!" said the big man, and he looked really shocked. "You look quite a nice little fellow, too— and yet you tell stories and steal bags. It is really shocking. Do you want me to call a policeman?"

"I think you must be mad," said Twiddle, holding on to the bag for all he was worth, for he felt quite sure the man would grab it if he could. "*I* shall call a policeman if you behave like this. I tell you this bag belongs to that old lady down the road there, and she left it behind in the grocer's —so I am running after her with it."

"You do tell big stories!" said the man. "Now look here—let's both go after that old lady, and if she says it's her bag, she can have it, and I'll say I'm sorry and go away."

"Well, that seems fair enough," said Twiddle, and they went after the old lady, who looked very surprised indeed when two men stopped her and spoke to her.

"Madam," said Mr. Twiddle, and he raised his hat very politely, "madam, you left your bag behind in the grocer's. Here it is."

The old lady looked at it and seemed puzzled. She didn't take the bag.

"Well, here it is," said Twiddle, impatiently, and held it out to her. She shook her head.

"I don't want it," she said. "It's not my bag!"

Twiddle stared at her as if he couldn't believe his ears. She pushed the bag away.

"I don't want it, I tell you," she said. "It isn't mine. I'm an honest old woman, I am, and I don't want things that are not mine."

She walked on, looking quite haughty. The big, burly man looked at Twiddle.

"There you are!" he said. "What did I tell you? It's all a made-up story of yours, isn't it? You saw the bag, picked it up, went off with it, and pretended you were taking it to the old lady when I found out you had it! I think you are a very bad fellow."

"I—I seem to have made a little mistake," said poor Twiddle, looking very hot and bothered. He gave the bag to the man. "Really, you must not think bad things of me, my dear sir. I belong to this town, and everyone knows me. I am a very honest and harmless fellow."

"Well, we'll see about that!" said the big man. "I'm going to see my sister's best friend to-day—and I shall ask her about you, and tell her what you've done. Yes,

166

this story shall go all round the town!"

"Who—who are you going to see?" asked poor Twiddle, hoping it wasn't Mrs. Gab, or Miss Gossip, for then surely everyone would know how silly he had been! Mrs. Gab and Miss Gossip spread all kinds of tales about.

"I'm going to see Mrs. Twiddle," said the man, "and a very good woman she is,

so I believe. My sister has often told me about her."

Poor Twiddle! He didn't know what to say. Then he cheered up. After all, Mrs. Twiddle was his wife and she loved him. Perhaps she would stick up for him. She often scolded him for things, but she knew he was kind and honest.

He didn't say any more but trotted back to the grocer's shop. He found his list on the counter and gave his order. He waited whilst everything was packed up. Then he went back home.

Now the big, burly man was there before him, and had already told Mrs. Twiddle about the bad, dishonest fellow who had taken his bag that morning. Mrs. Twiddle was shocked. "What was he like?" she said.

"Why—there he is—coming up your front path this very minute!" said the big man. "You be careful of him, Mrs. Twiddle. He may rob you, or deceive you with his tales."

Then the big man got a surprise. Mrs. Twiddle went very red. She looked as if she was going to burst. She picked up a broom and looked so fierce that the man was alarmed.

"You go out of my house at once," said Mrs. Twiddle. "Saying things like that about my Twiddle, who is the dearest, best, honestest—yes, and stupidest—fellow that ever lived. Take your bag and go!"

Twiddle heard all this—and he saw Mrs. Twiddle suddenly sweep with the broom

at the big man's feet. He laughed. How he laughed. Then he caught hold of Mrs. Twiddle and stopped her.

"Wait, my love," he said. "Don't send him away. I've been foolish this morning, and so has he. But it was worth it to hear you say all those nice things about me! Don't sweep the poor fellow off his feet!"

Mrs. Twiddle laughed. The big man laughed, too. Twiddle laughed the loudest. He shook hands with the man, and Mrs. Twiddle put the broom away.

"It's all turned into a good joke!" said Twiddle. "Now you just come and look at my garden whilst Mrs. Twiddle gets the dinner!"

Dear old Twiddle—he does get into muddles, doesn't he?

CHAPTER XV

MRS. TWIDDLE GETS CROSS

Mr. Twiddle sat in his chair reading the newspaper. Mrs. Twiddle sat by the fire, knitting. Click, click, click went her needles.

Mr. Twiddle sniffed. Mrs. Twiddle didn't say anything but she looked at him. He sniffed again.

"Don't," said Mrs. Twiddle. "Where's your hanky, Twiddle?"

"Don't know," said Twiddle, and sniffed again.

"But I gave you a clean one this morning!" said Mrs. Twiddle. "It must be in your pocket."

"Well, it's not," said Twiddle. "I've looked. I must have lost it when I went out for a walk. I remember taking it out once, but I don't remember putting it back into my pocket again."

"Now I shall have to give you *another* hanky!" groaned Mrs. Twiddle. "Anyone would think I was made of hankies!"

"No, they wouldn't, love," said Twiddle, looking at his plump little wife.

"Twiddle, I shall have to do something about your hankies," said Mrs. Twiddle, knitting very quickly, as she always did when she was cross. "You've lost five this week. Five!"

"Oh, no, dear," said Twiddle.

"Oh, *yes*, Mr. Twiddle!" said Mrs. Twiddle, and she rattled her needles loudly. "Five! It's got to stop. Next time you go out I shall pin your hanky inside your umbrella. Then you won't be able to lose it!"

"But it will be awfully difficult to blow my nose if my hanky is pinned inside my umbrella," said Twiddle.

"No it won't. You can put your umbrella up and the hanky will unfold and fall down to your nose," said Mrs. Twiddle. "You won't be able to leave it behind because it will be pinned to your umbrella. When you've used it you can just fold up your umbrella and put it down again."

"But have I got to put my umbrella up

every time I want to blow my nose?" said Twiddle, alarmed.

"Yes," said Mrs. Twiddle. "Then perhaps you will learn not to lose your hankies."

She was as good as her word. Next time poor Twiddle went out Mrs. Twiddle pinned his hanky firmly to the inside of his big umbrella.

"There!" she said. "Now you just can't *help* bringing your hanky home!"

Mr. Twiddle went out, hoping that he wouldn't have to blow his nose the whole afternoon. He couldn't bear the idea of putting up his umbrella every time he wanted to use his hanky.

Luckily he didn't want to blow his nose at all. He walked to the paper-shop, and then he went on into the country, meaning to sit on the stile he liked, and read his paper.

He soon came to the stile. He climbed up and opened his newspaper. He hung his umbrella on the top bar of the stile. Then he began to read.

The paper was very interesting. Although Mr. Twiddle had read almost exactly the same news in his morning newspaper it seemed just as interesting when he read it the second time. He read for so long that he forgot the time.

When he at last looked at his watch he was alarmed to see that it was almost tea-time.

"Now I shall be late for tea!" he said, and got off the stile in a great hurry. "Good

gracious! I must run."

So he ran, and just got home as Mrs. Twiddle was making the tea. "Late as usual!" she said. "Did you have a nice walk? Sit down. Tea is ready."

Twiddle felt very hot with his hurrying.

He panted. His forehead felt wet with heat, and he felt in his pocket for his hanky. It wasn't there, of course.

So he wiped his forehead with the back of his hand. Mrs. Twiddle saw him.

"Oh, Twiddle, where are your manners! Wipe your forehead with your hanky, do!"

"Haven't got it," said Twiddle, feeling in all his pockets again.

"Well, I pinned it inside your umbrella. Have you forgotten already?" said Mrs. Twiddle.

Mr. Twiddle got up to get his umbrella. But it wasn't in the hall-stand. How extraordinary. It was always there. But now it wasn't. What had happened to it?

And then, with an awful shock, Twiddle remembered that he had left it behind, hooked to the stile! Yes, he had hooked the handle to the top bar of the stile, with the hanky pinned in it—and he had left them both there! *Now* what would Mrs. Twiddle say?

"Perhaps I could pop upstairs and get another hanky before she notices anything

—and then after tea I could see if my umbrella is still on the stile," thought poor Twiddle.

But there wasn't any time to go and get a new hanky, because Mrs. Twiddle called out impatiently.

"Twiddle! What *are* you doing out there in the hall? Isn't your hanky in the umbrella?"

"Er—yes, my dear, it is," said Mr. Twiddle, thinking that it certainly must be.

"Well, bring it then," said Mrs. Twiddle. "You can surely unpin it?"

"Well—er—yes, love," said Twiddle, wondering how he was to unpin a hanky from an umbrella that wasn't there.

"I suppose your big clumsy hands can't undo the pin!" called Mrs. Twiddle, getting annoyed. "Bring the umbrella here then and I'll unpin the hanky. The scones are all getting cold. Dear, dear, I never knew such a man!"

Well, that was worse than ever. How could he bring in an umbrella that wasn't there?

"The umbrella isn't here," called Mr. Twiddle.

"Why not?" called back Mrs. Twiddle, puzzled.

"Well, I must have left it on the stile," said Mr. Twiddle, not daring to go back into the kitchen. But Mrs. Twiddle at once popped out into the hall.

"What! You've lost your umbrella now! You just put on your hat and go straight back to the stile and get it. Anyone might take it!"

So poor Twiddle had to leave his nice tea and go hurrying off to the stile. He was in such a flurry that he didn't notice Mr. Jinks hurrying in the opposite direction, carrying his umbrella with him. Mr. Jinks had passed by the stile and had seen the umbrella. He knew it was Mr. Twiddle's and now he was hurrying to take it back.

Twiddle didn't hear him calling. He just went panting on—and when he came to the stile, the umbrella wasn't there, of course.

So back went poor Twiddle, very much

afraid that Mrs. Twiddle would have a great deal to say to him that evening. He was very glad indeed when he saw his umbrella standing in the hall again!

"Mr. Jinks brought it back," said Mrs. Twiddle. "I gave him your scones to eat, in return for his kindness! But you can have bread and jam."

Now the next day Twiddle put on his coat to go out, and once more took his umbrella, which had his hanky still pinned inside. But Mrs. Twiddle called him before he went out.

"Twiddle! Come here a minute. Are you taking your hanky and your umbrella?"

"Yes, love," said Twiddle.

"Well, just to make sure you don't lose your umbrella again, I'm going to tie it to your coat-sleeve with thread," said Mrs. Twiddle. "Then, even if you do put it down and forget it, it will hang on to your sleeve, so you can't leave it behind. There now—that's tightly tied on, your hanky is pinned to your umbrella—and your umbrella is tied to your coat-sleeve—you can't possibly lose either of them now!"

Mr. Twiddle didn't at all like all this pinning and tying, but he didn't dare argue about it. Mrs. Twiddle was so much better at arguing than he was. So he set off, looking rather gloomy.

He thought he would go and look in at his old friend, Mr. Peto's. Mr. Peto had five children, and it was always a jolly house to go to. So he arrived at Mr. Peto's to find him playing an exciting game of rounders with the five boys and girls.

Now Mr. Twiddle loved rounders. He loved hitting out at the ball, and he liked trying to get somebody out. So he joined in the game too.

Soon he was feeling very hot, for he had on his coat. "Take off your coat, man, for goodness' sake!" said Mr. Peto, who had nothing on but shorts and a vest.

So Mr. Twiddle took off his coat and set it and the umbrella over the bough of a tree. Then he joined in the game. The sun came out and everyone got very hot.

"Lemonade, lemonade!" cried Mr. Peto, when the game was finished. "And ice-creams! Come on down to the village shop, all of you, and we'll drink lemonade and have ice-creams."

Mr. Twiddle liked lemonade and ice-cream too, so he went along, and he paid for a pink ice-cream for everyone. The children thought he was very kind.

Mr. Twiddle suddenly heard the village

clock strike one. He jumped up. "My gracious! I said I'd be home at half past twelve. I must fly. Good-bye!"

Off he went, thinking that it was very funny the way the time went when you were playing games. He came in at the door of his house, feeling rather late and flustered.

"Late again," said Mrs. Twiddle. "How hot you are! I hope you won't get a chill."

"A-tish-o!" said Twiddle, feeling for his hanky. It wasn't there, of course.

"Twiddle, you know your hanky is pinned to your umbrella," said Mrs. Twiddle, crossly. "Go and get it."

Twiddle went out to the hall to get it. His umbrella was not there.

"Now, don't tell me your umbrella isn't there, Twiddle!" called his wife. "I tied it to your coat, so that you couldn't leave it behind. Look for your coat, then for your umbrella, then inside for your hanky."

"Well, my coat isn't here," said Twiddle, desperately, "nor my umbrella, nor my hanky."

Mrs. Twiddle came out into the hall in

182

astonishment. "Well, where *is* your coat, then?" she said. Twiddle suddenly remembered.

"Well—dear me—yes, I must have left it hanging over the branch of the tree in Mr. Peto's garden," he said. "I was hot and I took it off. So the umbrella is there, too—and the hanky, of course."

Mrs. Twiddle stared at him. "Are you doing all this on purpose, Twiddle?" she asked sternly. "I suppose if I pin your coat to your vest you will come home without that too! You are a very annoying man. I shall not speak to you for the rest of the day.

This was the kind of punishment that Twiddle really enjoyed, because he thought that Mrs. Twiddle spoke far too much. But he pretended to look very sad. After his dinner, Mr. Peto brought back his coat, umbrella, and hanky and Mr. Twiddle thanked him very much.

"If you want to come to tea, you'd better come to-day," he said to Mr. Peto, "because Mrs. Twiddle isn't in a speaking mood, and we could have a nice quiet time."

"But, oh dear, Mrs. Twiddle overheard what he said, and that was the end of a nice quiet time! Poor Twiddle, he does get himself into trouble, doesn't he?